JULES SPENCER

PAYROLL

A NOVEL

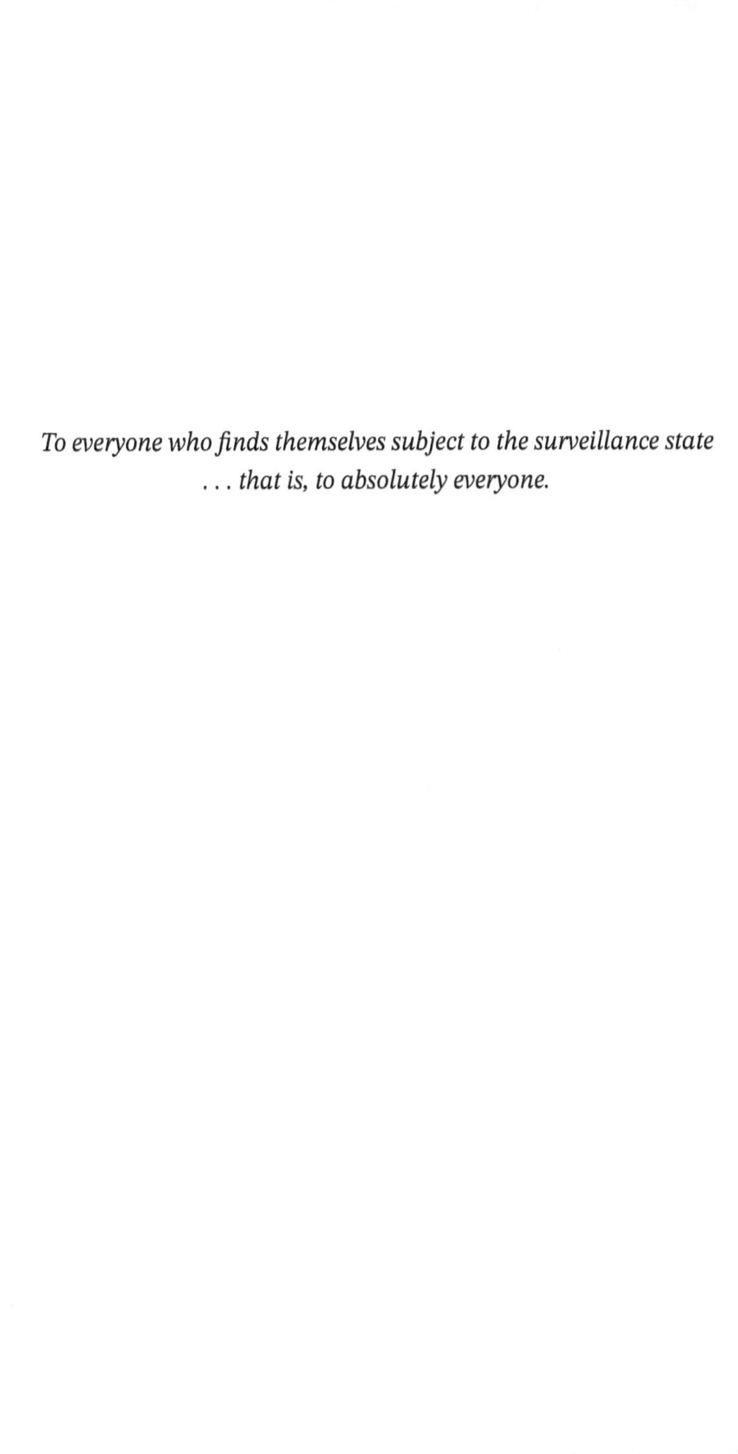

*To everyone who finds themselves subject to the surveillance state
. . . that is, to absolutely everyone.*

Sidewalk
Fiction Studio

PAYROLL

CHAPTER
ONE

THE ALARM BLARED in the darkness. Jenny groaned and groped around for her phone, her muscles still sore from the day before.

As she dressed in her uniform, she caught a glimpse of herself in the mirror—hair disheveled, eyes bloodshot, and a bruise forming on her shoulder from maneuvering heavy bags of coins. She climbed into her rickety car and went to work, where she parked the old sedan and found her armored truck for the day. She took a moment to adjust her black and blue uniform and check her reflection in the rearview mirror.

Jenny maneuvered the hulking truck through the early morning streets of Boston, its tires thrumming against the asphalt. Her mind drifted to the envelope of cash and valuables in the back, and how even a fraction of it could change her life.

She set her steeliest, hardest face and turned up the radio to drown out her thoughts.

The first pickup was at a jewelry store, the owner greeting her with a smile as he handed off cases overflowing with gold and diamonds. Jenny's back strained under the weight as she loaded them into the truck.

"Be careful with that one," the owner said with a wink. "Pure 24 karat."

Jenny resisted the urge to roll her eyes. What did he know about careful? His hands were soft, uncalloused. He sure looked like he'd never struggled to lift anything that outweighed him.

As she eased the truck down the road, its contents clinking and shuffling behind her, she thought of her empty apartment. Of the bills piling up on her table, the empty fridge.

She gave a chest-heaving sigh as she looked at the clock. Only two hours into her shift. She longed to go home, to collapse onto her lumpy couch and drown her aches in a hot bath.

She gripped the steering wheel tighter, navigating the truck down winding side streets. At least with the union dues and health insurance deducted, she earned a steady $18 an hour. It could be worse.

Could be worse, she reminded herself as the truck groaned to a stop outside another lavish building. Could always be worse.

An older man in a tailored suit greeted her at the entrance, eyeing her uniform with unveiled disdain.

"You're late," he snapped, thrusting a heavy bag at her chest.

Jenny bit back a sharp retort, years of practice keeping her tongue in check.

"Apologies, sir," she said instead, summoning a tight smile. "Boston traffic."

He sniffed and looked away, eager to be rid of her presence. The feeling was mutual.

Jenny turned on her heel and headed back to the truck, her fingers already numb around the bag's handles.

Just a few more hours, she told herself. A few more hours, and you can go home.

If only home felt like an escape.

Jenny's small frame belied the physical strength honed by years of hard work, and months of lifting heavy bags of money in and out of an armored truck. Standing at a mere five foot three inches, Jenny's wiry body carried the scars of her labor— a small burn on her left forearm from a previous gig in a kitchen, calloused fingers, and a perpetual ache in her lower back. But it was her face that captured people's attention: short, straight brown hair framed her delicate features, making her bright green eyes stand out against her ivory skin. A slight dimple graced her left cheek when she smiled, which wasn't often enough these days.

"Hey, Jenny!" called out Frank, another driver who had just finished his shift. "How we doing?"

"Same old, same old," Jenny responded with a wry smile, hoisting a bag onto her shoulder. "You know how it is."

"Tell me about it," Frank commiserated, wiping sweat from his brow. "Well, hang in there. At least we got a job, right?"

"Yep," she agreed, though her face betrayed the weariness that lay beneath her stoic facade. "At least we got that."

Halfway home, Jenny's car coughed, wheezed, roared, and stopped.

Under a cold, moonlit sky, she sat in her broken-down car on the edge of the street. The thin metal of the vehicle did little to protect her from the biting wind outside, and she shivered as she waited for the engine to cool. Her eyes darted between the rearview mirror and the empty road before her.

With a growl of frustration, Jenny forced herself to accept

the reality: her car had given up the ghost, and she was stranded. Her fingers drummed against the steering wheel in a rapid rhythm. She couldn't afford a rideshare, and she didn't want to ask her mother to come up all the way from Brockton.

But as the minutes dragged on and the temperature continued to plummet, Jenny's resolve crumbled. Finally, she fumbled for her phone with numb fingers and found her mom in the contacts list.

"Hey, Mom," she said, her voice cracking slightly. "I'm so sorry to bother you, but my car . . . it broke down. I don't have enough money for a cab . . . any chance you could give me a ride home?"

There was a pause on the other end before Ellen finally spoke. "Where are you, sweetie?"

"On Gallivan," Jenny replied, her gaze fixed on the dark horizon. "Just before the turn onto Neponset."

"Alright, hold tight. I'll be there as soon as I can."

"Thanks, Mom," Jenny whispered, swallowing the lump in her throat. As she hung up, she leaned back against the headrest, wallowing in guilt, gratitude, and worry.

Jenny watched as her breath fogged the windshield, the condensation reflecting the sickly yellow glow of a nearby streetlight. In a regression to childhood, she tried to distract herself by drawing in the fog on her window.

The anonymous hum of traffic on the road became suffocating. She felt at once invisible and exposed, the broke driver on the side of the road everyone notices and no one stops for. The darkness seemed to press in on her from all sides, heightening her sense of isolation. She started to imagine phantom footsteps echoing behind her, each one closer than the last. With every creak and groan of the metal carcass around her, Jenny felt her heart race faster.

"Get a grip," she muttered to herself, shaking her head in an attempt to banish her fears. "It's just a car. It's just a road. I'm a driver, for chrissakes."

Eventually, the headlights of Ellen's car shone in the rearview mirror, bringing relief. Despite her own grueling workday, Ellen hadn't really hesitated to drive all the way up from Brockton when Jenny needed her. The warmth in her mother's welcome as she opened the passenger door spoke volumes.

"Thanks for coming, Mom," Jenny said, exhausted as she settled into the familiar seat.

"Of course, honey," Ellen replied, her hands steady on the wheel.

As streetlights passed overhead, casting their fleeting glow into the car, Jenny found herself studying her mother's profile —strong, determined, and etched with the lines of years spent fighting to provide for her family.

"Did I tell you I decided to do one of those genealogy tests?" Ellen asked suddenly, breaking the silence.

"No, I don't think so," Jenny replied. "Anything interesting in the results?"

"No big surprises about where we come from or anything like that," her mother answered. "But there was one fun fact. They say we're related to someone named Elizabeth Cabot."

"Never heard of her," said Jenny. "Who was she?"

"Elizabeth was apparently the inspiration for one of the main characters in a kind of obscure novel by Upton Sinclair. I think the title was just *Boston*."

"Huh. Any idea what the novel's about?"

"I only found a Wikipedia on it," Ellen continued. "It was a mostly true story about two Italian anarchists, I think named Sacco and Vanzetti. They were framed for a robbery of two men bringing all the cash for payroll to a shoe factory. I mean, for murder, not robbery—the men carrying the payroll were shot and killed. But it all happened on the South Shore, like in Braintree, in the 1920s, I think. The anarchists didn't really commit the murder, but there was this big Red Scare at the time and the government wanted to frame these two because they were anarchists."

"But what does all that have to do with Ms. Cabot?"

"Some Bostonians were on the side of the anarchists, and our ancestor Elizabeth was one of them. I think the character based on her is called Cornelia. She went and worked in a rope factory in Plymouth and met these anarchists and some socialists there. Seems like she was a strong woman, someone who fought for what she believed in."

"Or she was a victim of a conspiracy theory, Mom," Jenny snorted. "A regular troublemaker. Sounds like about equal chances she was one or the other!"

"Don't be so cynical! We should find the book and read it before we judge, Jenny."

"Fair enough." Jenny gave in, resting one cheek on her hand and her elbow on the car's windowsill.

At home that evening, Jenny lay on her side, her body curled beneath the thin blanket as she stared unblinking at the shadows cast by the streetlights outside. Sleep eluded her as her mind raced with worry and frustration.

"I give up," she groaned, pushing herself up into a sitting position. With resignation in her eye, she reached for her phone, its screen casting a dim glow across the room.

She tapped at the screen, searching for the novel her mother had mentioned, but the fog she'd been in on the way home obscured her memory. She cast about blindly, searching for any details she remembered: "anarchists Braintree," "anarchists payroll heist," "anarchists framed murder Braintree." Finally the search gods—or demons—delivered a result that rang a bell. *Boston*, by Upton Sinclair.

Jenny's fingers moved with determination, tapping into obscure forums and navigating through digital archives. She stumbled upon a website claiming to have audio versions of rare, out-of-print books available for download. Sinclair's *Boston* came up.

"Finally," she muttered under her breath as she tapped on the link, initiating the download. What she couldn't see were the digital ripples that went out from her phone at the same time, traveling far beyond her little apartment in Quincy.

Jenny put on her headphones, lay back on the pillows, and pressed play.

At the FBI's Boston office, a few miles from Jenny's home, an alert popped up on the screen of a computer analyst. The analyst blinked in surprise, not expecting such an unusual flag on his radar. Pursing his lips, he forwarded the information to his superiors, suspecting that there might be more to this situation than met the eye.

"Check this out," he said, addressing a senior agent. "Someone just downloaded a dark-web version of a Sinclair novel called *Boston*. It's been flagged as extremist literature."

The senior agent raised an eyebrow, intrigued by the unexpected development. "What do we know about the person who downloaded it?"

"Name's Jenny Winters. Lives in Quincy. Seems like an ordinary person, but there's something odd about her searching for such an obscure book, and the search terms she used," the analyst replied, his curiosity piqued.

"Put her on the list," the senior agent instructed. "Let's see where this leads."

CHAPTER
TWO

THE OFFICE WAS DIMLY LIT, the fluorescent lights overhead casting a sterile pallor on the room. James Hartley, a rookie FBI agent, sat hunched over his desk, scrolling through files on his computer screen. His tall frame bent forward, tattoos peeking out from beneath his starched white shirt cuff. His short brown hair was tousled, and his deep brown eyes were intensely focused on the task at hand.

"Agent Hartley," a stern voice called out, cutting through the quiet hum of the bureau's offices. James looked up to find his boss, Agent Henry Thorn, standing in the doorway. Thorn was a stocky man with a buzz cut and an unwavering gaze that could pierce even the most hardened criminals.

"Sir?" James responded, straightening his posture and swiveling around in his chair to face his superior.

"Got a new assignment for you," Agent Thorn declared without ceremony, tossing a manila folder onto James's cluttered desk. "We've received intel on potential threats. Your assignment is to complete preliminary investigations on these individuals. Their online activity has raised red flags."

James flipped open the folder, revealing a list of names accompanied by their search histories and snippets of suspicious social media posts.

"Understood, sir. I'll get right on it."

"Good." Thorn paused, scrutinizing the young agent. "Remember, Hartley, we need to be thorough. These people may seem innocuous, but they could pose a real danger to our nation's security."

As Thorn withdrew from the room, James turned his attention back to the list before him. One name caught his eye: Jenny Winters, a 26-year-old armored truck driver from Quincy, Massachusetts. Her most recent search history contained inquiries about a payroll heist. His curiosity piqued, James began to delve deeper into her background.

"Jenny Winters," he muttered under his breath, as if speaking her name would reveal some hidden truth. He imagined the woman and wondered what drove her to these searches. Was it merely curiosity, or something more sinister?

Hartley knew that Jenny's occupation put her in a particularly interesting position with regard to the heist information she sought. He wondered about her intentions. As he sifted through the digital breadcrumbs of her life, he tried to remain objective, reminding himself that his duty was to investigate potential threats, not to judge, to condemn, or to invent compelling narratives.

Each new detail, each seemingly innocuous search, only served to heighten his interest in her story. Her financial struggles, her unassuming life—all these factors enticed the would-be hero within.

"Who are you, Jenny Winters?" he murmured as he traced her digital footsteps. "What are you planning?"

The clock's hands snapped along the circumference, their

ticks echoing in James Hartley's office as he pored over the list of potential targets. He sipped at the lukewarm coffee by his side, its bitterness grounding him in the task at hand.

His eyes were narrowed, focused, tracing lines across the screen, cross-referencing search histories with social media profiles. Each name on the list had their own story, their own secrets hidden beneath the surface.

Jenny's profile picture showed her smiling, the green of her eyes striking against the backdrop of a city skyline. The image did not match the troubling information he'd uncovered— Jenny's interest in a heist. As an armored truck driver, she would be intimately familiar with the ins and outs of armored vehicles and the security measures employed by the company. She would also carry a firearm, making her an ideal candidate to perpetrate such a crime.

Hartley's fingers danced across the keys once more, pulling up further details about Jenny's life: her family, her friends, even her favorite restaurants. In his mind's eye, he could see her walking along the streets of Quincy, her straight hair bouncing with each step, her laughter mingling with the hum of traffic.

The clock continued its steady march, and the sun dipped below the horizon, casting long shadows across Hartley's cluttered desk. A lone lamp illuminated the room, highlighting the concentration etched into his forehead as he delved deeper into Jenny Winters's past. The soft hum of the computer filled the space between the measured ticks of the wall clock. "Financial trouble," he muttered, scanning a detailed credit report. Jenny had been struggling for some time now, barely able to keep her head above water. The report was filled with late payments and collections notices. But it wasn't just money that troubled Jenny; Hartley's pulse quickened as he unearthed a criminal record. Shoplifting, disorderly conduct—minor offenses, perhaps, and at a very young age, but enough to paint a picture of a young woman teetering on the edge. She was desperate, vulnerable. Desperation was a powerful garden-variety motive for all kinds of crimes.

"Got it," he breathed, having found enough evidence to justify a deeper investigation. "Let's see where this trail leads, Jenny," he said softly. He seemed minimally cognizant of the moral gray area that came with his line of work, but he was clearly an aficionado of the thrill of the chase, the adrenaline that coursed through him as he closed in on the truth, or something like it.

He leaned back in his chair, allowing himself a moment to process this new information. It was an intriguing collection of facts, one that he would have to navigate with great care. But first, he needed to present his findings to Agent Thorn.

He knocked on the door to his superior's office. Henry Thorn looked up from his paperwork, his stern face betraying no emotion.

"Come in, Hartley," he said gruffly. "What do you have?"

"Sir, I've been investigating Jenny Winters, the armored truck driver," Hartley began, placing a thick folder on Thorn's desk. "I believe she may be planning a heist from her own truck, potentially motivated by leftist extremism."

"Go on," Thorn commanded, one eyebrow raised, his fingers drumming impatiently on the desk.

"Her online activity is suspicious, and she has a history of financial troubles. She also has a criminal record, sir." Hartley hesitated, his conscience wrestling with the weight of his words. "I think we should keep a close eye on her."

Thorn's eyes narrowed as he leafed through the report, stopping occasionally to scrutinize a particular detail. "I'll review your findings, Hartley," he said at last. "We'll discuss it further tomorrow."

"Understood, sir," Hartley replied, and with a nod, he took his leave.

Morning broke with an unremarkable grayness, casting a muted pallor across the city streets. The office was still quiet when Agent Thorn summoned Hartley back into his office. The creased lines of Thorn's face betrayed the gravity of his decision.

"Your report on Jenny Winters is thorough," he said, tapping the folder before him. "I'm giving you the green light to proceed with the investigation. But tread carefully, Hartley. Our mission is to serve and protect, not destroy. Remember your motto: fidelity, bravery, and integrity."

"Yes, sir," Hartley replied, his heart heavy with the responsibility now thrust upon him.

Hartley began his undercover operation by gathering more information on Jenny's daily routine and habits, her family and associates. As the shadows grew longer and the city melted into the twilight of a cold Friday night, he couldn't shake a gnawing feeling that time was running out.

MOLLY'S FINGERS fumbled with the edge of her coffee cup, sending ripples through the dark liquid. The awkward silence between her and Jenny at the kitchen table was decidedly out of the ordinary for a Saturday morning.

"Jenny," Molly finally murmured, "I . . . I lost my job again."

Jenny set her own cup down carefully, the warmth seeping into the grain of the wooden table. Her eyes held Molly's gaze.

"Again?" Jenny asked in disbelief. "What happened this time?"

"Same old story," Molly replied, waving a dismissive hand. "Boss didn't like my 'attitude,' whatever that means." Molly steeled herself and launched into the hardest part of the conversation. "Anyway, I can't afford the rent anymore. I'm moving back in with my parents."

The news hit Jenny like a gust of icy wind, making her shiver involuntarily. "Your parents?" Jenny echoed, attempting a casual tone even as panic clawed at her chest. "Are you sure? I mean, maybe we can figure something out . . . "

"Jen," Molly interrupted, shaking her head. "We've been over this before. I don't want to drag you down with me. I can't keep asking you to cover me. You'll be better off finding a new roommate."

The raw honesty in Molly's words stung Jenny, making her blink rapidly to clear the sudden blur in her vision. She clenched her fists beneath the table, a futile attempt to dissipate her frustration and fear.

"Okay," she finally replied. "I understand."

As Molly excused herself to the bathroom in an obvious attempt to avoid breaking down into tears herself, Jenny stared blankly at the chipped paint on the windowsill beside their table, her thoughts a whirlwind of dread and uncertainty. Her own job paid just enough for her to scrape by, but without Molly's contribution to the rent, she would have to find another way to make up the difference.

Her mind raced through a mental checklist of options: cutting back on groceries, canceling her gym membership, selling some of her stuff. But she couldn't think of a single possession that would be valuable to someone else, and none of these measures would be enough to bridge the gap between her income and the mounting bills that threatened to swallow her.

She stared out the window, searching for inspiration in the building walls layered in perspective down the street. "Think, Jenny," she whispered under her breath, bouncing her right leg in a frantic rhythm. With every anemic solution that flitted through her mind came the creeping realization that she was already sinking, and fast.

Jenny paced the scuffed hardwood floors that afternoon, clutching her phone in a clammy hand, her fingers tapping it restlessly against her leg, her thoughts a disordered jumble of troubles without any plans of attack attached. Her eyes dull with despair, she remembered her broken car, and remembered she hadn't gotten through to the shop yet to find out just how bad the damage would be. Her mechanic, Eddie, was not the most reliable about answering his phone.

"Come on, Eddie," she muttered under her breath as she dialed the mechanic's number for the third time. "Pick up."

"Eddie's Engines." Eddie Hanson crackled through the line at last. "How can I help you?"

"Hi," she began, with just a hint of a tremor. "My car was towed to your shop yesterday. The old red Accord. Have you had a chance to take a look at it yet? Can you let me know how much it's going to set me back?"

"Uh, yes. Jenny Winters, right? The '02 Honda?"

She confirmed.

There was a pause, filled by the rustle of paper on the other end before Eddie came back on the line. "I've got your estimate here. We're talking $2,000, maybe more. Your transmission's pretty shot."

"Two thousand?" Jenny's heart plummeted, her stomach twisting into a tight knot. "Eddie, I'm gonna be straight with you. I can't afford that right now."

"I get it," Eddie said, softening. "I don't do financing myself, but I know a guy. He does payroll loans—maybe he can help you out. It's not ideal, but it might buy you some time and get your car back on the road."

"A payroll loan?" she repeated, her eyes narrowing as she considered the implications. It was far from an appealing option—she knew all too well how quickly those interest rates could spiral out of control—but with her back against the wall, what choice did she have?

"Thanks, Eddie," she said at last, the weight of her predicament settling heavily on her shoulders. "I'll look into it. What's your guy's info?"

Eddie gave her the name and the number. "Thanks," she said, in a tone devoid of gratitude, ending the call and slipping the phone back into her pocket. A payroll loan. It left a sour taste in her mouth, but as she gazed out at the hodgepodge of buildings before her, the pinpricks of light winking through the people's windows like so many unattainable dreams, she gave up. She didn't have the will to sink into interminable internet searches for the cheapest loans. She would follow instructions.

Jenny's face flushed hot as she dialed the number for the payroll loan provider Eddie had recommended. She stared at the sun-faded curtains in her living room, the worn fabric a silent testament to the passage of time and the dinginess of everyday life.

"Hello, you've reached Fast Cash Payroll Loans. How may I assist you today?" The woman on the other end was jarringly cheery.

"Hi, I need to apply for a loan," Jenny said, barely above a whisper, as if saying it any louder would make the reality of her decision all the more unbearable. "Eddie Hanson referred me to you."

"Great! We can get you approved in just a few minutes." The representative rattled off a series of questions, each one prying further into Jenny's financial stability—or lack thereof. She divulged the necessary information, feeling exposed and vulnerable with each revelation.

"Alright, based on your information, we can offer you a

$500 loan against your next paycheck at an interest rate of 30 percent," the representative said, sounding almost too eager to help. "Would you like to proceed?"

"Thirty percent?" Jenny echoed, her eyes scrunched up, her hand on her forehead. But she believed she had no choice. She had more faith in her own powerlessness at that moment than anything else. "Okay, let's do it."

"Perfect! Just a few more details, and we'll have you all set up." The representative sounded positively chipper as she collected the final pieces of Jenny's personal and banking information. "You're all set, Ms. Winters. Your loan will be deposited into your account within the hour."

"Thank you," Jenny said, managing a weak smile she knew the representative couldn't see. She hung up the phone and swallowed the sour stomach feeling that crept up her throat with the knowledge of what she'd just done.

As the afternoon shadows deepened, Jenny sank into the couch and called Eddie back. "Hi Eddie, it's Jenny again. I got a loan for $500. Is that enough to start on the repairs?"

"Sure thing, Jenny," Eddie said warmly. "The result won't be perfect, but that'll be enough to do the essentials and get you back on the road. I'll start on it first thing tomorrow morning."

"Thanks, Eddie," she replied, her gratitude tempered by a sense of unease. She wondered if Eddie could hear the trepidation that lingered beneath her words, the unspoken acknowledgement that she'd just made a deal with the devil out of sheer desperation.

"Take care, Jenny. Let me know if there's anything else I can do for you," Eddie offered, before hanging up.

Jenny let the phone slip from her fingers, the plastic case sinking between the couch cushions as she stared into the ever-darkening room. She'd done what was necessary to survive another day, but the cost was like weights on her limbs, immobilizing her. A tiny spark of resistance caught hold; just enough to remind Jenny that she'd been inside in the stale air of the apartment all day long. She would take a walk. At least walking was still free.

CHAPTER
FOUR

THE EARLY MORNING sun crept through the blinds of Agent Hartley's apartment in Boston, casting a warm glow on his unmade bed. He sat on the edge, rubbing the sleep from his eyes before making his way to the small kitchenette. The coffee maker, set with clockwork precision, had just finished brewing a fresh pot of dark roast.

His thoughts were swimming with the task at hand: observing Jenny Winters, her daily routine, and habits. James knew he needed to blend in, remain invisible, and not arouse suspicion. He chose his clothing carefully—a worn navy hoodie, faded jeans, and a Red Sox hat, nondescript enough to go unnoticed in most places. A pair of old sneakers completed the ensemble, comfortable and quiet for walking.

Breakfast was a hurried affair—two slices of whole-grain toast smeared with strawberry jam, washed down with black coffee. The bitter, earthy notes invigorated him, setting his mind into sharp focus as he went over the details of his assignment once more. His heart raced with anticipation, a mix of excitement and fear reminding him of the delicate balance he needed to maintain.

Leaving the apartment, Hartley navigated the familiar streets of Boston and down 93 to Quincy with ease, his vehicle blending seamlessly with the steady flow of traffic. As he neared Jenny's building, he scoped out a discreet spot to park, where he could observe the entrance without being noticed. Sipping from his thermos of steaming coffee, he settled in for the long haul—watching, waiting, listening.

The church bells echoed through the quiet neighborhood, their solemn chimes punctuating the still air. It was in these moments that Hartley felt the weight of his role, the invasive nature of his surveillance. The knowledge that Jenny had no privacy, no sanctuary from his watchful gaze, gave him a feeling of power. He observed the comings and goings of her neighbors, attempting to piece together the intricate puzzle of their lives, searching for any clue that might lead him closer to the truth about Jenny Winters.

Hartley's car was bathed in early morning light, making it crucial for him to maintain his vigilance. The camera nestled in his lap, he kept his finger on the shutter, ready to capture any significant moment.

Jenny and her roommate Molly emerged from the building together, deep in conversation. Hartley quickly snapped a few photos of them, capturing their expressions and body language as they walked down the street toward a coffee shop. What was their relationship like? Were they confidantes or merely roommates sharing space out of necessity? He already knew Jenny didn't have a sister, and her cousins lived in Brockton and other towns farther down on the South Shore. When the two returned with coffees and breakfast sandwiches, he documented their laughter, the ease with which they navigated each other's presence, before they disappeared back into the building.

Minutes later, a young man stepped out, shielding his eyes from the sun as he scanned the area. Hartley tensed, watching the lanky figure approach a pickup truck before climbing into the driver's seat and moving it, positioning the bed of the truck at the rear door of the apartment building. The agent sensed something unusual about this maneuver and took several more photographs, trying to glean any insight into Jenny's possible connection to this man.

Realizing that his current position provided limited visibility of the rear entrance, Hartley decided it was time to change perspectives. He started his car, driving around the block in search of a better vantage point. But as he suspected, there were no suitable parking spots available.

Frustration mounted within him, but he knew that if he wanted to keep a watchful eye on the back door of the building, he would have to adapt. Returning to his original spot, he exited the car and slung a messenger bag over his shoulder, concealing the camera and other surveillance equipment within. He donned his baseball cap, adjusting it to partially obscure his face before slipping on a pair of sunglasses.

Meticulously scanning the area once more, Hartley began walking toward the back of the building, taking care to blend in with the morning joggers and dog walkers. His heart raced as he moved closer, knowing that one false step could jeopardize his entire operation. As he neared the rear entrance, Hartley identified a small park across the street—a perfect location for covert observation. Settling onto a bench, he positioned himself so that the morning sun cast long shadows, further concealing his presence. From here, he could monitor the comings and goings at the back door without arousing suspicion.

Hartley's eyes narrowed as he watched the tableau unfold before him. Jenny, Molly, and a young man emerged from the rear entrance of the apartment building like well-rehearsed actors on a stage. The scene was laden with an air of urgency, and Hartley felt the tension mounting within him.

The man's tall, lanky frame appeared almost comically juxtaposed with the cumbersome boxes and suitcases he hauled out into the sunlit alley. His shaggy blonde hair, damp with perspiration, clung to his forehead as he worked. Jenny and Molly moved in tandem, their petite forms dwarfed by the bulky items they carried. Even so, they managed the task with a grace that suggested familiarity.

Hartley surreptitiously snapped photos of the trio, documenting the number, size, and shape of the boxes. He wondered what secrets lay within those cardboard walls. Were they related to some illicit activity, or merely the trappings of ordinary life? His instincts whispered that there was more to this seemingly mundane scene than met the eye.

As the last box found its place in the bed of the young man's pickup truck, Hartley observed a moment between Molly and Jenny. Their arms entwined in a long, tender embrace, the women seemed to forget the world around them for a fleeting instant. He could see the subtle quiver of Jenny's lips, the way she tried to suppress the emotion that threatened to overwhelm her.

When they finally pulled apart, Jenny turned and retreated back into the building, her hand surreptitiously brushing away a stray tear that had escaped her defenses. It was a small detail, yet it spoke volumes about the depth of her connection with Molly. Watching the intimate exchange, Hartley considered the nature of their relationship and the role it might play in his investigation.

"I'll need to dig deeper," he mused, tucking his camera away as he made a mental note to delve into the associates' backgrounds. They were pieces of the puzzle that was Jenny Winters, and Hartley was determined to uncover how they fit together.

As the truck rumbled to life and pulled out of the alley, its cargo secure, Hartley prepared for the next phase of his operation. He retreated to his vehicle, hands shoved deep into his pockets against the bite of the cold air. He needed a moment to regroup and reevaluate his plan; with two subjects now out of sight, he couldn't afford to lose track of Jenny as well.

Seated behind the wheel, he rubbed his hands together briskly, cursing the frigid metal casing of his camera. It was in these quiet moments that Agent James Hartley reveled in the thrill of the chase—the uncertainty, the unknowns, the challenge of piecing together the fragments of a life under the weight of suspicion. Every move Jenny made, every word she spoke, was a tantalizing clue waiting to be deciphered.

"Stay focused, Hartley," he whispered to himself, eyes locked on the entrance of the apartment building. Time seemed to stretch, the hands of his watch advancing at a glacial pace.

Then, without warning, the front door swung open and Jenny emerged, a large laundry bag slung over her shoulder. The sight of her, weighed down by her burden yet still graceful in her movements, stirred something within him—a strange, inexplicable pull that tugged at the edges of his consciousness.

"Damn it," he muttered under his breath, shaking off the feeling as he fumbled for the ignition. He shouldn't be feeling anything for her, least of all attraction. But there was no denying the allure of her bearing, the way she seemed to see straight through him even from this distance.

As he followed her slowly down the street, his grip tightening on the steering wheel, he found it impossible to tear his gaze away from her. She moved like a ghost, her footsteps barely audible above the crunch of frostbitten leaves beneath her feet. And yet, despite her apparent sadness, there was a resilience about her that he admired in spite of himself.

"Could she be disposing of evidence?" he wondered, the thought sending a shiver down his spine. He dismissed it as unlikely—after all, what kind of criminal would take the time to fold their incriminating material neatly into a laundry bag? But if there was one thing Hartley had learned during his time with the Bureau, it was never to underestimate the cunning of those who lived in the shadows.

As Jenny continued her slow progress, it became clear that following her by car was no longer viable. The drone of the engine was too intrusive, too conspicuous; he needed to blend into the background, become part of the scenery. With a sigh, he pulled over and killed the engine, watching as Jenny's figure diminished further down the street.

"Here goes nothing," he murmured, stepping out of the car and onto the sidewalk. Tugging the collar of his coat higher around his neck, he set off in pursuit, his pace measured and unhurried.

James shadowed Jenny from a distance, the crisp autumn air biting at his cheeks as he trailed her through Quincy's somber streets. As she pushed open the door to a laundromat, the overhead bell chiming her arrival, James paused for a moment before following suit.

Once inside, he pretended to check on a load of laundry—someone else's, a tiny deception in a day filled with lies. His eyes flickered between the dryer's spinning contents and Jenny, attempting to catch a glimpse of what she was placing into the washing machine. It appeared bulky, but the view was obscured by her small frame, and he couldn't quite make out the details.

A man, unkempt and leering, sidled up to Jenny, invading her personal space with an unsettling grin. James tightened his grip on the stranger's laundry basket, feeling the plastic dig into his fingers as he fought the urge to intervene. He watched as the man attempted to flirt with Jenny, who responded with a steely glare that spoke volumes.

He could just make out Jenny's terse reply to the man's unwelcome overtures: "Mind your own business." The man, undeterred, spat an insult at her, his words dripping with venom. James's protective instincts flared, but he knew he couldn't afford to draw attention to himself. With reluctance, he tore his gaze away and made his way toward the exit, stepping out into the chill of the morning.

Across the street, he found a spot shrouded in shadows, offering him a clear view of the laundromat's entrance. He leaned against the cold brick wall, watching as Jenny, now alone once more, continued her task. The man's unwanted advances had left her visibly on edge, and James felt a pang of sympathy for her—as well as a growing sense of admiration for her strength.

As Jenny eventually emerged from the laundromat, her movements now lighter and more carefree, James tensed in anticipation. He knew he would have to resume his pursuit soon, but something held him back for a moment longer. The door swung open once more, and the creepy man stepped out into the fading light, his gaze scanning the street like a predator in search of prey.

When the man's gaze locked onto Jenny, now some distance away, James felt his stomach clench with anxiety. He watched as the man set off after her, his intentions all too clear. James's heart raced as he watched the man from the laundromat stalk Jenny from a distance. He knew he couldn't intervene directly without blowing his cover, but he couldn't stand idly by and allow her to be harassed or worse. As they approached a narrow alley lined with overflowing dumpsters, inspiration struck. He noticed a group of pigeons pecking at crumbs scattered across the pavement. With careful precision, James picked up a rock and tossed it into the midst of the birds.

The pigeons took flight in a flurry of feathers and startled coos, drawing the creepy man's attention away from Jenny for just a moment. But that was all James needed. He swiftly darted toward the man, using the chaos as cover, and bumped into him forcefully.

"Watch where you're going!" James snapped, feigning anger while concealing his true purpose.

"Get lost," the man growled back, momentarily distracted from his pursuit of Jenny.

"Learn some manners, jerk," James retorted, turning his back on the man and walking away, hoping his ruse had been enough to deter him from following Jenny any further. Glancing over his shoulder, he saw the man scowl and change direction, stalking off in the opposite way, thwarted for now. Relief washed over James, but he felt that he'd stepped over a line somehow in his relationship to the subject of investigation.

James watched Jenny approach her apartment building. She seemed unaware of the danger she had narrowly avoided, her movements graceful and unhurried. He found himself captivated by her every step, the way her hair caught the fading light, and the curve of her shoulders beneath her coat.

Jenny entered her building, and James returned to his vehicle. After another couple of trips to the laundromat, Jenny returned home and stayed there for the rest of the afternoon. James took out his binoculars and shifted his focus to her apartment window, which had begun to glow with warm, inviting light. From his vantage point, he could see her moving about the kitchen, preparing her evening meal. He tried to maintain a clinical detachment as he took notes in his notebook. The intimate details of Jenny's life unfolded before him like a play on a private stage—the way she paused to sip her wine, her look of concentration as she read a recipe, and the fluid dance of her hands as she chopped vegetables. Each small act seemed charged with a strange significance for James, who felt an unexpected tenderness swelling within him.

"Focus," he muttered under his breath, attempting to quell the rising tide of emotion that threatened to overwhelm him. But even as he admonished himself, his gaze was inexorably drawn back to the window, where Jenny stood illuminated against the encroaching darkness. The night wore on, and James continued his vigil, the light from Jenny's apartment a constant presence in the periphery of his vision. He watched as she moved from room to room, her figure framed by each illuminated window like a living tableau. He was drawn to her, a moth to her flame.

Finally, late into the night, Jenny's lights began to blink out one by one. James held his breath as he watched her bedroom window darken, the shadows swallowing up her form as she retreated into sleep. Only then did he allow himself to exhale, the tension in his chest easing ever so slightly.

With Jenny safely tucked away for the night, James gathered his notes and equipment, preparing to return to his own home. As he drove through the deserted streets of Quincy, his thoughts kept circling back to Jenny—to the way she had stood at her kitchen window, to the curve of her neck as she bent over her recipe book, to the strength that seemed to radiate from her every movement. He shook his head, trying to dislodge the images that threatened to consume him.

Once home, James wasted no time in poring over the information he had collected during his surveillance. Each detail, meticulously cataloged and cross-referenced, formed an intricate structure of connections that slowly began to reveal the hidden patterns of Jenny's life. Though he couldn't yet see the full picture, James knew that he was getting closer to uncovering the truth—whatever it may be.

As he worked, James found himself grappling with an unfamiliar sense of unease. The more he delved into Jenny's world, the more he felt as though he were intruding on something sacred, violating a trust that had never been granted him. He tried to remind himself that this was what he had been trained for, that this was necessary in order to bring criminals to justice. But the words rang hollow in his ears, drowned out by the memory of Jenny's face, soft in the dim light of her apartment.

"Damn it," he muttered, slamming his pen down onto the table. "What the hell is wrong with me?"

As dawn bled into the sky, casting a pale light over the city, James sat in his apartment, surrounded by the evidence he'd gathered on Jenny Winters. Despite the creeping exhaustion that clawed at him, his mind raced with possibilities, each new lead branching out like creeping ivy. He traced the patterns of her life, connecting seemingly unrelated fragments to form a picture that was both fascinating and disturbing.

The silence of his apartment weighed heavily upon him, pressing down on his chest as if to suffocate any lingering doubts about the morality of his actions. He knew he should be proud of the progress he had made so far, but instead, he found himself consumed by an unfamiliar emotion—guilt.

"Focus," he told himself sternly, shaking his head to clear away the distraction. He studied the photos he'd taken and the detailed notes about her daily routine. There were still gaps in the puzzle, missing pieces that eluded him despite his relentless pursuit. But as he sifted through the accumulated data, he felt certain that the answers were within reach, tantalizingly close yet just beyond his grasp.

CHAPTER
FIVE

JENNY HAD JUST STEPPED out of her apartment building the next morning, squinting against the sunlight, when a familiar figure sauntered toward her. Max Thompson, her pothead neighbor and occasional supplier of good conversation, carried two steaming cups of coffee and a brown paper bag from which wafted the tempting scent of freshly baked delicacies.

"Morning, Jenny," he drawled, nodding in greeting as he handed her one of the coffee cups and the paper bag. "Thought you might like a little something to start your day."

"Thanks, Max," she replied cautiously, her eyes flickering with suspicion as she sipped the coffee. It was strong, just the way she liked it. "This is unexpected. What's the occasion?"

"Can't a guy do something nice for his neighbor without an ulterior motive?" Max said lightly, but she could see the curiosity lurking beneath his casual demeanor.

"Of course," she said, taking a bite from the muffin she found inside the bag, and raising one eyebrow.

"Alright, you got me," Max admitted after a pause,

scratching at his scruffy beard. "Ever since we helped Molly move out, I realized I haven't seen your car in the lot . . . Just wanted to check in, see if you're alright."

"Appreciate the concern, Max," Jenny answered, keeping her tone neutral. "But I can handle myself."

"Never doubted it for a second," he grinned, before casting her another curious glance. "You think Molly will still come over and hang out? We're going to miss her around here."

"Ask her yourself! Now, if you don't mind, I've got to get going. My car's supposed to be ready at the shop," Jenny said briskly, tossing the remains of her muffin into a nearby trash can and striding off toward the bus stop.

"Alright, take care," Max called after her, still watching her with those inquisitive eyes. "And if you need anything, you know where to find me."

Jenny nodded without turning around. As she waited for the 220 bus, she found herself mulling over her interactions with Max. He seemed genuinely concerned about her well-being, but there was something else lurking beneath the surface, a curiosity that bordered on intrusive. She couldn't shake the feeling that he had an ulterior motive.

The bus wheezed along the streets to Quincy Center, where Jenny waited again, this time for the 230, which finally dropped her off near Eddie's Engines just as the clock struck 10:00 a.m. As Jenny walked through the open garage doors, she saw Eddie Hanson, the owner of the shop, wiping his hands on a rag as he approached her.

"Morning, Jenny," he greeted her gruffly, his well-built frame towering above hers. "We just got some news about your car. Sorry I didn't get a chance to call you before you came all the way here."

Jenny's face fell.

"Your car needs some new parts," Eddie explained, gruff and to the point. "We've got a new guy working on it, Sean Collins."

Jenny's gaze drifted across the garage floor, past the scattered tools and half-assembled engines, until it settled on a tall figure stooped over an engine block. The man, presumably Sean, had a lean, muscular build that was accentuated by his tight-fitting work clothes. His dark hair was swept back from his angular face, which was smudged with grease but still managed to convey an arresting handsomeness. Jenny felt an unexpected jolt of attraction as she took in his strong jawline and the curve of his bicep beneath his rolled-up sleeve.

"Sean!" Eddie called out, causing the young mechanic to glance up from his work. His eyes met Jenny's, and he gave her a smile that made her heart skip a beat.

"Hey there," Sean said as he approached, wiping his hands on a rag much like Eddie had done earlier. He extended a hand toward Jenny, and she grasped it firmly, feeling its surprising softness, so different from the calluses on Eddie's hands.

"Nice to meet you, Jenny," he continued, smooth and confident. "I'm Sean, the new mechanic here. I've been working on your car."

"Hi," she replied, trying not to let her attraction show too obviously. "Nice to meet you." She shifted her weight from one foot to the other, the coffee cup in her hand threatening to tip precariously. As she tore her gaze away from Sean's face for just a moment, she noticed a particularly interesting tattoo peeking out from beneath his shirt sleeve. It seemed to be a complex intertwining of gears and cogs, a fitting design for a mechanic.

"Can you tell me what's wrong with my car?" Jenny asked, attempting to sound casual as she leaned to the side to get a better look at his tattoo. In her distraction, she tilted the coffee cup just enough for the scalding liquid to slosh over the rim and onto her hand.

"Ah!" she yelped, dropping the cup and clutching her now-burning hand to her chest. Coffee splattered across her shirt and then the concrete floor, leaving a dark, steaming stain.

"Are you okay?" Sean immediately stepped closer, concern etched into the lines of his face.

"Y-yeah," Jenny stammered, flustered by the combination of pain and embarrassment. "Just a little spill."

"Let me grab some ice for your hand," Sean offered and disappeared into a back room.

As Jenny waited for him to return, she tried to regain control of her emotions, berating herself for letting a little chemistry throw her off balance. It didn't help that her hand still throbbed painfully from the burn, but she was determined not to let it show when Sean returned.

"Here," he said, handing her a small plastic bag filled with ice. "Hold this against your hand—it should help with the pain."

Jenny pressed the bag of ice against her reddened hand, wincing as the cold seeped into her skin. The sharp contrast in temperature seemed to heighten the burn's sting rather than alleviate it. Sean hovered nearby, his concern evident in the way he kept glancing at her hand, then back up to her face.

"My bad, I didn't even think to get you a towel," he said, striding over to a workbench cluttered with tools and rags. He grabbed a cloth, not noticing the dark smudge of grease staining one side.

"Here, hold still," he instructed gently, reaching out to dab at the droplets of coffee splattered across Jenny's shirt. His fingers grazed her collarbone, and she felt an involuntary shiver run down her spine. The sensation was electric, pulling her gaze up to meet his.

Their eyes locked, and for a moment, time seemed to slow. There was an intensity to Sean's gaze, a depth that hinted at something more than mere concern. A sudden heat flickered behind his eyes, mirroring her own disquiet.

"Uh, sorry," Sean muttered, abruptly breaking eye contact and stepping back. "I didn't mean to, uh, touch you like that."

"It's fine," Jenny replied quickly, trying to regain her composure. She glanced down at her shirt, only now noticing the streak of oil smeared across the fabric. "Oh . . . looks like I've got some grease on me too."

"Damn, I'm sorry about that," Sean apologized, looking rattled. "I didn't realize there was oil on the rag. We can try to clean it off if you want?"

"No worries, I'll take care of it at home," Jenny said, forcing a small smile. "I think I've had enough excitement for one day."

"Right, of course," Sean agreed, rubbing a hand along the back of his neck. "I'll just, uh, go get the notes on your car, then."

"Thanks." Jenny watched as he retreated toward the garage, feeling an odd mixture of disappointment and relief at his departure. She knew she should be more focused on her car, but her mind seemed to be stuck on the way Sean's fingers had felt against her skin, the intensity of his gaze.

Sean emerged from the back of the garage, wiping his hands on a clean rag. He approached Jenny with an air of professionalism, but she could still see something else lingering in his eyes. "About your car," Sean said, turning his attention to a clipboard he held. "We had to order some parts. It will take about a week or so for them to arrive." Jenny felt a pang of disappointment at the thought of being without her car for that long, but she knew there was little she could do about it.

"Is there any way to speed up the process?" she asked, unable to keep the hope from her question.

"I'm afraid not," Sean answered, shaking his head. "But I can assure you we'll get your car fixed as soon as possible."

"Thanks," Jenny said, trying not to let the frustration show on her face.

"Listen," Sean began, hesitating for a moment as if unsure how to proceed. "If you have any concerns, or if you just want an update, here's my number." He scribbled it on the corner of a sheet of paper on the clipboard and tore it off, handing it to her.

"Feel free to call me directly," he added, his eyes meeting hers once more. "Any time." The intensity of his gaze sent a shiver down her spine, and she found herself wondering what secrets lay hidden behind those dark eyes.

"Thank you, Sean," Jenny said, pocketing the slip of paper. "I appreciate it."

"Of course," he replied with a small smile. "We'll do our best to get you back on the road as soon as possible."

As she turned to leave the shop, Jenny glanced back at Sean one last time. The bus stop was a short walk from Eddie's Engines, and Jenny found herself trying to ignore the dampness of her coffee-stained clothes as she waited under the shelter of a weathered awning. Her breath formed small clouds of condensation in the chilled air, and she pulled her coat tighter around her, feeling the shape of Sean's number in her pocket.

"230 to Quincy Center," came the automated announcement as the bus groaned to a halt in front of her. The hiss of the doors opening snapped her out of her thoughts, and she mechanically tapped her CharlieCard before finding a seat near the window. The vehicle lurched back into motion, its engine rumbling low like a giant cat's purr.

"Can't believe I have to wait another week for my car," Jenny muttered under her breath, watching as the streets rolled by outside her window. The world seemed muted, the colors dull and washed out, as though the gray sky had bled into everything it touched.

"Excuse me?" A woman in her forties, clad in a worn peacoat and clutching a canvas tote, looked at her curiously from the adjacent seat.

"Sorry, just talking to myself," Jenny replied, forcing a tight-lipped smile. She turned her gaze back to the window, but the woman continued to watch her, an unspoken question hanging in the air between them.

"Car trouble?" the woman finally ventured, breaking the silence as Jenny felt the weight of her stare.

"Something like that," Jenny said, rubbing her forehead. "Just found out it'll be another week before I can drive it again."

"I know how that feels," the woman commiserated. "My car broke down two years ago. Here I am, still taking the bus. It's not the most convenient, but you get used to it."

"Thanks," Jenny said. She appreciated the woman's attempt at solidarity, but it did little to alleviate her stress and made her feel self-conscious about complaining when most of her fellow passengers probably didn't have a car.

As the bus continued on its route, stopping and starting every few blocks, Jenny found herself thinking of Sean. His unexpected kindness and the charged moments they'd shared seemed like a small light amid the dreariness. The idea of calling him stirred in her a mix of trepidation and excitement, emotions she hadn't felt in quite some time.

"Last stop, Quincy Center," the automated voice announced, pulling Jenny from her reverie. With a sigh, she rose from her seat, balancing herself as the bus jolted to a halt. As she stepped off onto the pavement, she couldn't shake the feeling that something had shifted within her—a subtle, but undeniable change.

CHAPTER
SIX

JENNY SAT on her worn-out couch, phone in hand, as she scrolled down to Molly's number. She pressed her phone to her ear, waiting for the call to connect.

"Hey, Molly," she said when her ex-roommate finally picked up.

"Jenny!" Molly said cheerily. "What's up?"

"I was actually wondering if you could do me a favor," Jenny said. "Could you give me a ride to work tomorrow? My car's still in the shop."

"Of course," Molly agreed without hesitation, her loyalty to Jenny shining through. "I'll be there bright and early."

"Thanks, Molly." Relief washed over Jenny, her shoulders dropping from their tense position. "You're a lifesaver."

"Speaking of work, I've been dealing with this unemployment mess," Molly said. "I'm worried that my old boss will tell the agency I was fired for cause, and then I won't be able to get any benefits."

Jenny leaned back into the lumpy cushions, recalling Molly's similar concerns in the past. "You were worried about the same thing last time, remember? But it worked out just fine."

"Ugh, yeah," Molly groaned. "But the red tape was insane. I had to jump through so many hoops to keep those benefits coming."

As they talked, Jenny studied the peeling wallpaper on her living room wall, following the intricate patterns. She felt a pang of sadness at the thought of losing this place, but pushed it aside, focusing on the conversation.

"Maybe it's time to think about what kind of job you really want," Jenny suggested gently. "Something that would make you happy."

"Happy?" Molly scoffed, a hint of her sarcastic humor slipping through. "At work? I don't even know what that looks like anymore."

"Come on, there has to be something," Jenny urged, a smile tugging at the corners of her mouth as she imagined the possibilities for her friend. "Maybe something creative? Or something where you get to help people?"

Molly sighed, but Jenny could hear the faintest hint of hope. "I don't know, maybe you're right. It's worth thinking about, I guess."

"Definitely," Jenny encouraged.

"So, tell me what's been going on with you." Molly changed the subject. "Anything new?"

Jenny hesitated before diving into the story of her encounter with Sean, the mechanic. "Well," she began, "I had an interesting experience at the mechanic's shop." She described Sean to Molly in vivid detail, from the rugged handsomeness of his face to the way his muscular arms flexed.

"Anyway," Jenny continued, "I managed to spill my coffee

all over myself, like the klutz I am, and he was nice enough to help clean up the mess. And then he gave me his number."

"His personal number?" Molly repeated, her tone incredulous. "You mean not just the shop's number?"

"Right," Jenny confirmed, a hint of uncertainty creeping in. "And now I can't stop thinking about him. I'm tempted to call or text him, but I'm nervous because, well, I'm actually attracted to him."

Jenny could feel her cheeks growing warm as she confessed her feelings to Molly, and she quickly added, "Do you think it's normal for mechanics to give out their personal numbers? Or do you think maybe he's interested in me too?"

Molly let out a low whistle, clearly impressed by the turn of events. "Honestly, Jen, mechanics don't usually hand out their numbers like candy," she said, laughter lacing her words. "There's definitely something going on there."

"Really?" Jenny's heart skipped a beat, hope and excitement mingling together inside her chest.

"Absolutely," Molly assured her, her tone teasing yet sincere. "In fact, I'd say it's a pretty clear sign that he's into you."

"Maybe I should contact him then," Jenny mused, her fingers twitching with anticipation as she toyed with the idea.

"Go for it!" Molly encouraged, her enthusiasm infectious. "What have you got to lose?"

"Okay, so let's say I do decide to text him," Jenny said with a mixture of excitement and trepidation. "What should I even say? I don't want to come off as too eager or anything."

Molly leaned back in her chair, the creak of the wood through the phone line punctuating her thoughts. "Well, you could always ask something about your car. That way, you're not making it obvious that you're interested in him, but you're still opening up the conversation."

"Right, right," Jenny murmured, considering the suggestion. Her gaze drifted to the window, where the afternoon sun dappled the walls with shifting patterns of light and shadow. The world outside seemed muted, as if holding its breath as she weighed her options.

"Or," Molly continued, her tone conspiratorial, "you could say you found a great coffee place nearby and thought he might like to try it out. You know, since you guys met when you spilled your coffee and all."

Jenny laughed at the idea, the sound ringing through the room. "That's actually pretty clever," she admitted, her heart warming at the thought of sharing a cup of coffee with Sean. "It's casual enough that it doesn't scream 'date,' but it's still kind of cute and flirty."

"Exactly," Molly agreed, brimming with satisfaction. "So, are you going to do it? Are you going to text him?"

"Maybe," Jenny hedged, a flicker of uncertainty crossing her features. "I just need to work up the courage first."

"Trust me, Jen, if there's one thing you've got in spades, it's courage," Molly said. "You can do this."

As they continued to discuss potential conversation starters, Jenny felt a growing sense of anticipation. She knew that reaching out to Sean was a risk—there were no guarantees when it came to matters of the heart—but the idea of taking that leap together held a thrill she couldn't quite resist.

Their conversation was suddenly interrupted by a knock on Jenny's door, the sound jarring her from her thoughts. "I've got to go, Molly," she said, an apologetic smile touching her lips. "Someone's at my door."

"Alright," Molly acquiesced, with a touch of curiosity. "But don't forget about what we talked about, okay? Don't be too shy to call that handsome mechanic of yours."

With one last chuckle, Jenny ended the call and crossed the room, her steps echoing softly on the hardwood floor. Jenny got up on tiptoes to look through the peephole; to her surprise, Max stood before her door, his frame hunched slightly, his hair framing his face in a way that made his eyes seem even more vibrant. There was an air of uncertainty about him that Jenny couldn't quite place.

"Hey there, Max," she said. "You do know Molly moved out, right?"

A faint blush bloomed on Max's cheeks as he rubbed the back of his neck nervously, an endearing gesture that betrayed his usual confident demeanor. "Yeah, I know," he admitted, his gaze flicking around the room behind her before settling on her face once more. "Actually, I came to see you."

"Me?" Jenny raised an eyebrow, intrigued by this unexpected turn of events. Her heart thrummed in her chest, sending a subtle shiver down her spine.

"Uh, yeah." Max shifted his weight from one foot to the other, appearing somewhat sheepish. "I was wondering if you wanted to come over to my place and watch the Celtics game tonight."

The words hung in the air between them, glistening with potential. Jenny studied Max for a moment, noting the way his fingers toyed with the hem of his faded band tee, betraying his unease. She watched as he swallowed hard, his Adam's apple bobbing in his throat.

"I just thought it'd be fun, you know? A chance to hang out and relax."

Jenny hesitated for a moment, searching his face for any

hidden intentions. Max seemed genuine enough, and she had to admit that some company would be nice.

"Sure, why not?" she finally answered, attempting to sound nonchalant. "I'd love to join you."

Max's eyes widened and a grin spread across his face, transforming him from a picture of nerves into one of pure elation. "Great! I'll see you later then?"

"Definitely." With that, Jenny closed the door, leaving Max in the hallway, the sound of his retreating footsteps echoing in her ears.

Jenny leaned against the cool wood, her fingers tracing the grain as she mulled over the unexpected invitation. Curiosity played on her features, lips pursed in bemusement. It had always seemed as if Max's affections were directed toward Molly, yet here he was, asking her to join him for an evening. She wondered if there was more to this newfound interest than met the eye.

Shaking off her thoughts, Jenny decided to embrace the opportunity, allowing herself to indulge in the thrill of the unknown. Pushing away from the door, she moved through her apartment with purpose. In the kitchen, she glanced at the sink filled with dishes from her hurried breakfasts and late-night dinners, an untidy reminder of her hectic life. With a sigh, she rolled up her sleeves, grabbed a sponge, and began to scrub.

As the soapy water sloshed against the sides of the sink, Jenny hummed a tune she remembered from her childhood— a simple melody that had once brought her comfort after long days spent navigating the complexities of adolescence. It felt appropriate now, as she found herself grappling with the unexpected turns her life had taken.

The suds swirled like tiny galaxies around her fingers, and

for a moment, Jenny allowed herself to forget about her financial woes, focusing instead on the burgeoning excitement within her. Sean, the mechanic with the easy smile and kind eyes, flitted into her thoughts alongside Max, her enigmatic neighbor who might have a secret crush. The prospect of romance with either—or both—of them sent a thrill down her spine, leaving her torn between them.

Her mind continued to dance between Sean and Max, weighing the possibilities as she rinsed off the last dish and placed it in the drying rack. As she wiped her hands on a dishtowel, the buzzing anticipation grew stronger, making her heart thud a little harder in her chest.

Determined to make the most of the evening, Jenny went to her bedroom and scanned the contents of her closet for the perfect outfit. She pulled out a few different options and held each one up to her reflection in the mirror, mentally envisioning how they would look on her petite frame.

"Okay, Jenny, think casual, but cute," she muttered under her breath, carefully considering each item. After some deliberation, she settled on a soft, slightly oversized sweater and a pair of well-fitted jeans.

As she dressed, the anticipation continued to build within her, fueled by the knowledge that, for once, fate seemed to be shining on her. The weight of her worries and struggles seemed to lessen, replaced by the fluttering excitement of new beginnings and unexpected connections. And as Jenny looked at herself in the mirror, a faint smile playing at the corners of her lips, she started to feel that, perhaps, things were finally starting to look up.

With a last, lingering glance in the mirror, Jenny took up her curling iron and set to work. She deftly twisted strands of her short hair around the heated wand, adding gentle waves that softened her features and framed her eyes. The hiss of the curling iron filled the small room, accompanied by the faint scent of warm ceramic and the quiet hum of her own thoughts.

She set the curling iron aside, allowing her newly-styled locks to cool as she moved on to her makeup. A light dusting of eyeshadow accentuated the natural depth of her eyes, while a swipe of mascara elongated her lashes, the dark pigment contrasting strikingly with her fair skin. Finally, she dabbed a subtle rose-tinted gloss on her lips, completing the look.

Standing back from the mirror, she appraised her handiwork. The overall effect was understated yet alluring—she had struck the perfect balance between looking put-together and approachable. Pleased with the result, she reached for her perfume, a delicate floral scent that lingered in the air like the ghost of an embrace. As it settled on her skin, mingling with her natural warmth, she felt a renewed sense of confidence.

Her mind raced with anticipation, but she pushed those thoughts aside for now. There were more pressing matters at hand, like finding something suitable to bring over to Max's apartment. Crossing back into the kitchen, she swung open the refrigerator door, only to be confronted by a disheartening sight: near-empty shelves, devoid of any beer or snacks that might make for suitable offerings.

"Damn," she muttered under her breath, her good mood momentarily faltering. But then, inspiration struck. With a sudden burst of hope, she yanked open the freezer, revealing two frost-covered pizzas tucked away amidst the icy depths. Her smile returned, brighter than before.

"Better than nothing," she said to herself, gingerly prying the pizzas from their chilly embrace. She slipped them into a grocery bag, grabbed her purse, and stepped out of her apartment. She made her way down the building hallway, the scent of old carpets and stale air filling her nostrils. It was a familiar smell, one that had become almost comforting to Jenny in her time living there.

As she made her way down the stairs, the soft echoes of her footsteps mingling with the distant murmur of neighbors going about their lives, she marveled at the unpredictability of life. Only a short while ago, she had felt as if the world was conspiring against her—a never-ending cascade of setbacks and challenges that threatened to overwhelm her completely.

But now, as she walked those familiar steps toward Max's door, she felt a strange sense of exhilaration. The future stretched before her like an undiscovered country, teeming with possibilities and potential—and for once, she found herself eager to explore it.

"Who knows?" she whispered as she reached the landing. "Maybe things are finally starting to turn around."

CHAPTER
SEVEN

JENNY HESITATED at Max's door, the wood grain and chipped paint beneath her fingertips feeling both familiar and new. She paused, listening to the faint murmur of a television beyond the barrier, and in that moment she felt something stir within her—a delicate fluttering that danced along her nerves like the brush of butterfly wings. It was excitement, anticipation, and yes, even a hint of fear that sent a shiver down her spine.

"Here goes nothing," she whispered, and raised her hand to knock.

"Come in!" came Max's voice, slightly muffled by the door but no less warm for it. The sound of his invitation bolstered Jenny's resolve, and she pushed the door open, stepping into the cozy sanctuary of Max's apartment.

"Hey, Jenny! I'm glad you could make it," Max beamed, his eyes brightening as he looked up from the coffee table where he'd been arranging an array of snacks. "You didn't have to bring anything, but I appreciate it."

"Consider it my contribution to game night," she replied

playfully as she held up the grocery bag with a flourish, offering him a glimpse of the frozen pizzas inside. "I hope you like pizza."

"Absolutely," Max grinned, his enthusiasm genuine, and Jenny felt a warmth spread through her chest. She watched as he took the bag from her and busied himself with preheating the oven, noting the way his fingers fumbled with the dials, betraying a hint of nervousness.

"Nice place you've got here," she said, surveying the comfortable clutter of his living room—the stacks of books and magazines, the worn but inviting couch that faced the TV. It was a space that spoke of a life lived with gusto, and she felt drawn to it.

"Thanks," Max replied. "I've been here for a few years now. It's not much, but it's home. Can I get you a beer?"

"Sure, thanks," she replied, settling into the worn cushions of the couch with a contented sigh.

The television flickered to life, the sound of the announcers filling the room as they discussed the anticipated game. The Celtics were playing their long-standing rivals, the Miami Heat. A tension hung in the air, even miles away from the arena, as fans from both sides awaited the start of the game.

"Here you go." Max handed Jenny a cold bottle, condensation beading on its surface. Their fingers brushed briefly in the exchange. The fleeting touch sent a shiver through Jenny, and she wondered if he felt it too.

"Thanks," she murmured.

When Max re-emerged from the kitchen, oven timer set, he flopped down on the couch beside Jenny. His proximity sent a shiver down her spine, though she tried her best not to let it show. Instead, she took a swig of her beer, savoring the bitter taste as it slid down her throat.

"Should be a great game tonight," Max said, leaning back and stretching his arm casually along the back of the couch behind Jenny. She could feel the heat radiating from his body, his scent—a mixture of earthy cologne and something uniquely him—filling her nostrils.

"Definitely," Jenny agreed, trying to focus on the screen as the players took their positions.

As the game progressed, the atmosphere in the room grew more relaxed as the beers flowed freely. Each time one of them got up from the couch, they sat a little closer when they returned. Soon their bodies brushed against one another with every cheer and groan that escaped their lips. The air between them crackled with a palpable tension, a current that pulsed beneath their skin and sent shivers down their spines.

"Did you see that shot?" Max asked in a whisper as he leaned in closer, the warmth of his breath tickling Jenny's ear. She nodded, still watching the screen, but her senses were heightened—every movement, every sound seemed amplified, sharpened to an almost unbearable degree.

"Unbelievable," she murmured, feeling the thrum of her heartbeat echo through her chest and into the pit of her stomach. Her fingers tightened around the neck of her beer bottle, the condensation cold and slick against her skin.

"Want another?" Max offered, his arm brushing hers as he rose from the couch. She hesitated for a moment, weighing the decision in her mind, before nodding her assent. "Sure, thanks."

As Max disappeared into the kitchen, Jenny's gaze drifted around the room, taking in the stacks of books and records, the worn posters that adorned the walls, the collection of knickknacks and mementos that spoke to a life lived fully and passionately. It was a side of him she had never seen before, a glimpse into the inner workings of his heart and mind—a priv-ilege she found herself coveting more than she wanted to admit.

"Here you go," Max said as he handed her a fresh bottle. Their eyes met for a moment, and Jenny felt the heat rise in her cheeks, a silent acknowledgement of the delicious tension between them.

"Thanks," she whispered, looking away as she took a sip, the bitter taste of the beer grounding her, tethering her to the present.

"Anytime," Max replied soft and low, a secret shared only between them. He settled back onto the couch, their knees brushing against one another's as the game played on.

"Maybe this is just the beginning," Jenny thought, her pulse quickening at the endless possibilities that lay ahead. "Who knows," she mused, her heart swelling with anticipation and hope, "maybe tonight is the night everything changes."

CHAPTER
EIGHT

UNDER THE FLICKERING fluorescent lighting of the FBI office, James Hartley stood with a 20-page report clenched in his hand. He felt an unexplained and unexpected pang of guilt as Jenny's face flashed through his mind.

Shaking off the feeling, he reported to Thorn's office.

"Agent Thorn," James said, forcing himself to stay focused on the task at hand, "here's my report on Jenny Winters."

Thorn extended his hand without taking his eyes off the computer screen. His fingers brushed against the edge of the report, causing it to tremble slightly in James's grip.

"Thank you, Agent Hartley," he said curtly, finally tearing his gaze from the screen to take the report.

As Thorn began scanning through the pages, the lines on his brow deepened, casting shadows across his features. The silence stretched out, making the hum of the office equipment seem deafening to James. He watched Thorn look back and forth across the pages, searching for any sign of progress or breakthrough.

"Let's hope this pans out, Hartley," Thorn said finally,

setting the report down on his desk. "I don't want to see our resources wasted on a dead-end case."

"Sir," James began, his voice level and determined, "I believe there are some key pieces of evidence here that warrant further investigation." He tapped the report on Thorn's desk for emphasis. "Phone records show regular contact with known criminal elements, and her bank statements reveal a sudden influx of funds."

Thorn raised an eyebrow, unimpressed. "And how exactly did you obtain these, Hartley?"

"Surveillance, sir. I've been keeping tabs on Jenny around the clock, both in person and through electronic means."

"Is that all?" Thorn asked, his tone dripping with skepticism. "You've given me nothing but circumstantial evidence, Hartley. This is hardly grounds for a full-scale operation."

James clenched his jaw, struggling to maintain his composure under Thorn's relentless scrutiny. He knew his superior was a hard man to please, one who demanded results and had little patience for anything less than perfection. But James couldn't shake the feeling that there was something more to Jenny's story, something hidden beneath the surface of her seemingly mundane life.

"Sir, I understand your concerns, but I truly believe we're onto something here. If we can just give this case a little more time—"

"Time is a luxury we cannot afford, Agent Hartley," Thorn interrupted, his tone rising in volume and intensity. "We have bigger fish to fry, and I cannot justify allocating resources to chase after a small-time player like Jenny Winters. If you don't find anything more significant, we'll have to drop it, much as I would love to put a communist in the defendant's seat."

Disappointment swelled in James's chest like a lead weight.

He knew Thorn was right—there were more dangerous criminals out there, individuals who posed a far greater threat to society than a struggling armored truck driver from Quincy who may or may not harbor leftist political beliefs. But he couldn't shake the nagging feeling that there was some hidden truth just waiting to be uncovered.

"Understood, sir," James replied. "I'll continue to monitor her activities and report back with any new developments."

"See that you do," Thorn said, dismissing him with a curt nod.

The sterile white walls of the hallway seemed to close in on James as he walked away from Thorn's office, each step heavier than the last. The fluorescent lights above hummed their disapproval, casting harsh shadows that only served to deepen the lines etched in his face.

"James!" a woman called out, bright and vibrant against the tension. Turning his head, he saw Lauren Bernard striding toward him, her ebony curls bouncing with each step, a smile like a sunburst adorning her face.

"Lauren," he greeted her, attempting a smile but feeling it fall short.

"You two look like you just had a thrilling conversation," she said, with a nod toward Thorn's office as she approached. "Let me guess—another lecture on the importance of surveillance techniques and the evils of the criminal underworld?" Her tone was light, teasing, but there was an edge to it that belied her awareness of the pressure they both faced.

"Something like that," James replied, his lips quirking up into a half-smile. "Though I think my case might have been the primary subject of scorn today."

"Of course. Jenny Winters, the enigma wrapped in a mystery, shrouded in a cloud of exhaust fumes," Lauren quipped. "I've heard whispers of your exploits, Agent Hartley. Word has it you've been getting all kinds of cozy with our elusive quarry."

"Hardly," James retorted, his manner dry as the desert, though he could feel the heat rise in his cheeks. He knew she meant no harm, but her words struck a chord within him. "Just doing my job, same as you."

"Of course, of course," she responded, her hands raised in mock surrender as they walked back to their desks. "Though I must say, if your job includes getting up close and personal with the suspects, you might want to let me in on your secret. My last assignment had me chasing down a cranky old counterfeiter whose idea of a good time was watching reruns of *Wheel of Fortune*."

"Believe me," James said, his tone serious despite the humor in his expression, "there's nothing glamorous about it. Sometimes, the closer you get to someone, the harder it is to see them for who they really are."

"Speaking of challenges," Lauren began, "I've been hitting a few brick walls with my own case. I swear, tracking down this arms dealer is like trying to catch smoke with your bare hands."

"Sounds like you've got your work cut out for you," James replied, genuinely interested in her struggles. He watched as she toyed with a ballpoint pen in her slender fingers, the subtle movement catching the light and casting fleeting shadows across her face.

"Tell me about it," she sighed, "I've been chasing leads from Boston to New York and back again. It's like playing a game of cat and mouse where the mouse has a jetpack and you're stuck wearing clogs."

"The joys of fieldwork," he commiserated, shifting his gaze

from her hands to the stack of papers on his desk. "At least you don't have to worry about getting grease stains all over your reports."

"True," she laughed, and for a moment, the tension in the room seemed to dissipate. "But I'd trade a dozen ink smudges for the chance to see your face when you realized you had to stake out a truck driver."

"Would you now?" he asked, arching an eyebrow as he leaned closer, his tone low and teasing. "Well, I must admit, there's something to be said for getting to know the ins and outs of a vehicle. In fact, I think it's made me a better investigator."

"Really?" she asked, a mixture of amusement and curiosity playing at the corners of her mouth.

"Absolutely," he affirmed, allowing himself a small smile as he met her gaze head-on. "You see, much like an armored truck, a person can be full of complex and interconnected systems. You've got to know how to read the signs, listen for the subtle cues that tell you what's really going on under the hood."

"Interesting metaphor," she conceded, her lips curving into a wry grin. "I suppose I'll have to take your word for it, seeing as my last undercover gig involved posing as a librarian."

"The notorious Dewey Decimal System," he deadpanned, enjoying the easy rapport between them. "A formidable foe, to be sure."

"Indeed," she agreed, her laughter a balm to his frayed nerves. "So, do I need to watch my back, Agent Hartley? Are you gunning for my spot as top rookie?"

"Wouldn't dream of it," he assured her, his words laced with good-natured sarcasm. "After all, who am I to challenge the reigning queen of witty repartee and razor-sharp investigative instincts?"

"Flattery will get you nowhere, James," she warned playfully, but the appreciative glint in her eyes betrayed her true feelings.

"Good thing I'm not trying to get anywhere," he shot back, his tone light and teasing. "Just stating a simple fact."

With a flick of her wrist, Lauren nonchalantly dismissed James's flirtatious compliments. "Enough about me," she said coolly, the playful glint replaced by the steely resolve of an agent who knew her priorities. "Focus on your case. What's your next move with Jenny?"

James admired her ability to switch gears so seamlessly, even as he felt a pang of disappointment at her deft redirection. "Good question," he mused aloud. "I'm still working on that."

"Come on, James," she chided gently, as if coaxing a recalcitrant child. "You're not one to shy away from a challenge. Use that big brain of yours."

"Maybe I could borrow some of your legendary wit and intuition?" he quipped, leveling a mock-pleading gaze at her. "After all, it seems to be serving you well."

"Nice try," she countered, flashing him a knowing grin. "But you'll have to find your own way through this particular maze."

"Fair enough," he conceded, the corners of his mouth lifting into a wry smile. "I suppose I can't expect to ride your coattails forever."

"Indeed not," she agreed, before shifting her focus back to the case file in James's hand. "Now let's get back to work, shall we? Have you considered tracking her financials more closely?" Lauren suggested, her eyes narrowing as she took the report and scanned it.

"Already on it," James replied, a hint of pride coloring his tone. "But nothing's come up yet. She's been careful."

"Or perhaps she's simply not involved," she countered with a fusion of skepticism and smugness.

"Always the contrarian, aren't you?" he retorted with a grin, refusing to rise to the bait. "Even when it comes to your own colleagues' investigations?"

"Only when I sense there's something amiss," she replied cryptically, her gaze meeting his in a silent challenge.

"Then let's hope my instincts prove sharper than yours," he said softly, his gaze never wavering from hers as they shared a moment of charged silence.

"Speaking of instincts," Lauren said, "it might be wise to trust yours a bit less when it comes to flirting with coworkers."

"Flirting?" James feigned shock, his eyes widening in mock surprise. "I was merely expressing my admiration for your skills as an investigator."

Lauren chuckled, shaking her head. "You're as transparent as those interrogation-room windows, Hartley."

As their playful banter reached new heights, Thorn leaned against the doorframe of his office, his arms crossed over his chest. His stern gaze bore into the back of James's head like a drill.

"Agent Hartley," Thorn barked, causing both James and Lauren to startle. "Your focus should be on your investigations. Save your charm for the subjects."

"Of course, sir," James replied, his cheeks flushing with embarrassment as he hastily gathered his report from Lauren's grasp.

"Agent Bernard," Thorn addressed Lauren, his tone softening ever so slightly, "continue your work on the arms trafficking case." He paused, his expression hardening as he added, "And I expect both of you to put personal matters aside while on duty."

"Understood, sir," they chorused, subdued and chastened.

With a final nod of disapproval, Thorn turned and closed his door. The room seemed to shrink under the weight of his departure, the air heavy with the unspoken tension that lingered between James and Lauren.

"Guess we'd better get back to it," Lauren murmured, her earlier levity all but vanished. She offered James a small, apologetic smile before returning to her desk and immersing herself in the labyrinth of case files that awaited her.

James watched her for a moment, his heart heavy with regret. He knew he had overstepped, allowing the camaraderie between them to eclipse the seriousness of their tasks. It was a mistake he couldn't afford to make again.

"Good luck with your case," he said softly, his words barely audible above the hum of the office machinery. Lauren didn't respond, her focus seemingly unbreakable as she delved further into her investigation.

With a sigh, James turned back to his own work, his thoughts consumed by Jenny and all the things surrounding her that didn't quite add up. As he pored over the evidence once more, he felt the weight of Thorn's disappointment bearing down on him. He knew he needed to uncover the truth, to prove his worth as an agent—but at what cost? None of the other names on the intel list had panned out; Jenny was his only good lead.

As the fluorescent lights continued to cast their harsh glare upon the agents' diligent efforts, the shadows grew long and the clock ticked relentlessly onward, each second bringing them closer to the precipice of discovery—or failure.

CHAPTER
NINE

MOLLY'S OLD CAR, a rusted blue sedan that had seen better days, idled outside Jenny's workplace. The paint was flaking in parts and the driver's side mirror hung on by sheer willpower. A thick layer of grime coated the windows, as if it were trying to keep the secrets within from escaping. Jenny approached the car, squinting through the fading light of the evening.

"Nice ride," she said sarcastically as she opened the passenger door. The creaky hinges protested against her intrusion.

"Hey, be nice to her," Molly retorted, pushing aside a heap of discarded fast-food wrappers and empty soda cans to make room for Jenny. "She may be old, but she gets me where I need to go. And you know what they say about beggars and choosing."

Jenny wrinkled her nose at the pungent odor that wafted up from the mess: stale grease mixed with the sharp tang of old cigarette smoke. She gingerly lowered herself into the seat, careful not to touch anything sticky or unidentifiable.

"Your car smells like a frat house after a wicked kegger," Jenny quipped, rolling down the window to let in some fresh air.

"Very funny," Molly replied, rolling her eyes. "Now put on your seatbelt. This baby isn't getting any younger." As they pulled away from the curb, Molly launched into recounting the events of her day.

"First, I took Grandma to the salon. You wouldn't believe the gossip those old ladies share. Quincy at its finest. Then, Mom roped me into helping her clean the house. Honestly, it wasn't too bad. But I spent most of the afternoon searching for jobs online, and man, is that depressing."

"Did you find anything promising?" Jenny asked, genuinely curious.

"Maybe," Molly sighed. "I'm thinking about trying to find a new career altogether. Something with stability, you know? I'm tired of having no job protection. My next gig has to be a union job."

"Union jobs do offer better protection," Jenny concurred, watching the passing scenery outside. "Can't blame you for wanting that." The car rumbled along, the groan of the engine struggling against the weight of years of neglect.

"Anyway, enough about my day," Molly said, changing the subject. "How was work?"

"Work was . . . well, work. You know how it is." Jenny paused, taking a deep breath before recounting her day. "One of the trucks had a flat tire today, which set us back a couple of hours. Then, my manager wanted to have a 'chat' about my punctuality. As if I control traffic. One pickup in the Seaport and my whole day is off." She rolled her eyes and sighed, the weight of her long day evident in the slump of her shoulders.

Molly glanced over at Jenny and decided to steer the

conversation toward something lighter. "So, what's going on in the old building lately? How are all the neighbors?"

"Well, as it happens, I spent some time with Max the other night," Jenny replied. The faintest blush crept up her cheeks as she spoke.

"Really?" Molly raised an eyebrow, a playful smile appearing on her face. "Do tell."

"Nothing scandalous, I assure you," Jenny retorted defensively. "We just hung out in his apartment for a bit. Frozen pizza, beer, and a Celtics game." She looked away from Molly, focusing on a lone streetlamp casting its glow over the darkened road.

"Sounds cozy," Molly teased, her expression evolving into a wide grin. "You sure you're not harboring a little crush on our dear neighbor Max?"

"Please," Jenny scoffed, trying to maintain her air of indifference. "It was just a friendly evening, nothing more."

"Alright, alright," Molly relented, still grinning. "But you have to admit, he's cute in that scruffy hipster sort of way."

"Maybe," Jenny allowed, the ghost of a smile playing at the corners of her lips.

"But speaking of Max," Jenny said, her tone casual as she studied the passing scenery outside the car window, "I still think he's more interested in you than me. Honestly, nothing really happened that night."

Molly scoffed, amused by the thought. "Oh, come on. I'm pretty sure Max has had a thing for you since forever."

"Really? What makes you say that?" Jenny asked, genuinely curious.

"Alright, let me give you an example," Molly began, recalling a vivid memory. "Remember that time when we had that barbecue party in the building's courtyard last summer?

You were over at the grill, flipping burgers and chatting with everyone. And there was Max, just standing off to the side, holding a beer and watching you with those puppy dog eyes."

Jenny chuckled at the mental image. "Okay, fair enough. But what about this: remember when we had that power outage and you were stuck groping around in the pitch-dark stairwell? Who arrived with a massive flashlight and led you to safety? Max."

"True," Molly conceded, her fingers drumming against the steering wheel. "But then there was the time you got locked out of your apartment. He didn't hesitate to help you pick the lock, even though it took hours and he had plans that night."

"Fine," Jenny relented, smirking slightly. "But how about the time you had that flat tire, and he insisted on changing it for you, even though it was wicked early in the morning? He seemed pretty invested in making sure you were taken care of."

Molly sighed, unable to argue with that. "You've got a point there. But still, all those moments could have just been him being a good neighbor, right?"

"Maybe," Jenny replied, unsure herself. "Or maybe he's just really good at hiding his true feelings."

"Okay, okay," Molly said with a wave of her hand, cutting off Jenny's latest story. "Maybe neither of us really knows what's going on in that guy's head." She frowned for a moment, the car's headlights slicing through the darkness as they continued down the street. "But honestly . . . is Max even boyfriend material?"

"Excuse me?" Jenny raised an eyebrow, her eyes glinting with curiosity.

"Think about it," Molly said thoughtfully. "Sure, he's sweet and helpful, but does he even have goals for his life? He just seems to be coasting, not really aiming for anything."

Jenny pursed her lips, considering Molly's words. It was true that Max appeared content with his somewhat aimless existence, never expressing any desire to change or grow.

"Then again," Molly added with a self-deprecating chuckle, "I'm not exactly one to talk about having career goals, am I?"

"True," Jenny admitted. "But at least you're actively trying to find something new, right?"

"Maybe," Molly shrugged, her gaze fixed on the road ahead. "Anyway, back to Max. No one really knows what he does for a living or how he makes his money. I mean, we've all heard rumors, but nothing concrete."

"Right," Jenny agreed, her expression growing serious. "It's kind of unsettling, if you think about it. We know so little about him, yet we trust him enough to let him help us out with personal stuff. Makes you wonder what his real intentions are."

"Exactly," Molly said, her fingers tapping against the steering wheel in time with the rhythm of their shared doubts.

The car fell silent as both women pondered this new angle, the shadows outside seeming to deepen and twist into sinister shapes.

"Maybe we're overthinking this," Jenny said hesitantly. "Perhaps he's just a genuinely nice guy who happens to be a little mysterious," Jenny murmured, her gaze drifting out the window at the passing buildings.

"Jen . . ." Molly began, but her words were drowned out by the sudden blaring of a ringtone.

"Sorry," Jenny muttered, her cheeks flushing with embarrassment as she fumbled to silence the phone. She glanced at the screen, reading the caller ID—Sean Collins. She hesitated, her thumb hovering over the answer button.

"Go on," Molly urged, sensing her friend's uncertainty. "Take the call."

Reluctantly, Jenny swiped right, bringing the phone to her ear.

"Hello?"

"Hi, Jenny. It's Sean Collins from the repair shop. I'm sorry to call so late," he said warmly with a hint of apology. "I wanted to let you know there's been an additional delay in getting the parts for your car. They were backordered, so we have to get them from another supplier."

"Oh," Jenny replied, her disappointment evident in the slight falter of her voice. "That's . . . unfortunate." Her fingers tightened around the armrest, the frustration bubbling beneath her polite tone. She knew she needed to keep her composure; after all, it wasn't Sean's fault that her car was falling apart.

"Look, I feel terrible about this," Sean continued, sensing her thinly veiled dismay. "How about I make it up to you with dinner? My treat."

Jenny hesitated, the offer unexpected and tempting. She considered the implications and weighed them against her desire to save face. Her stomach rumbled in agreement, making the decision for her.

"Alright," she relented, a hint of amusement coloring her words. "A free meal would certainly be helpful, considering I'm spending all my money on car repairs."

Molly's eyes widened in horror at Jenny's joke. She frantically waved her hands, signaling for Jenny to stop talking about being broke. Jenny's cheeks flushed a deep shade of crimson, and she stammered, trying to backtrack.

"Uh, I mean, it's just that car repairs can be expensive, but it's not like I'm actually broke or anything," she stumbled over her words, hoping her embarrassment wasn't too obvious.

Sean gave a friendly laugh. "How about Friday night? Seven thirty?" Sean asked, his enthusiasm palpable through the phone, seemingly unfazed by her sudden awkwardness.

"Friday works," Jenny agreed, her heart fluttering at the prospect of a proper meal and pleasant company. She couldn't deny that the idea was appealing, even as she chastised herself for her fanciful thoughts.

"Perfect, I'll pick you up." There was a note of excitement in Sean's tone, the promise of an enjoyable evening hanging in the space between them. "Just text me your address."

"Okay! See you then," Jenny said.

"Looking forward to it!" Sean replied. "Goodnight, Jenny."

"Goodnight, Sean," she said before hanging up, her heart still pounding from the near disaster.

As soon as she ended the call, Molly burst into laughter. "Oh my god, Jenny, I've never seen anyone shoot themselves in the foot so fast!" She bent over the steering wheel, clutching her stomach with one hand as laughter overtook her.

"Shut up," Jenny grumbled, her face still burning with humiliation. "It was just a stupid joke. I didn't think he'd take it seriously."

"Of course he'd take it seriously! You don't joke about being broke when you're talking to a potential date," Molly lectured, wiping tears of mirth from her eyes. "You really need to work on your flirting skills."

"Thanks for the expert advice, single girl," Jenny shot back, trying her best to maintain some semblance of dignity. The streetlights cast their glow upon the sidewalk, creating pools of light amidst the growing shadows.

Molly snickered, shaking her head in disbelief. "You know, there's an art to flirting, and you, my friend, have much to learn."

"Whatever," Jenny muttered, rolling her eyes, even as a small smile tugged at the corners of her lips.

"For real, though," Molly continued, her laughter subsiding as they turned down the familiar streets to their apartment building. "You need to be more careful with what you say. Guys like Sean don't come around often, and you don't want to scare him away."

"Thanks, I'll keep that in mind," Jenny mumbled, thinking there might be some truth in Molly's words.

"Okay, but seriously," Molly said, "what do you think of Sean? Do you think he's got potential?"

Jenny's cheeks burned, not just from the cold, but from the sudden scrutiny her love life, such as it was, was under. She glanced out the window, searching for words. "Well, he's polite and hardworking. And he's trying to make amends for the delay with my car, so that's something."

"Right," Molly mused. "But what about the spark? The chemistry? You can't build a relationship on politeness alone, you know."

Jenny sighed. "I'm not sure yet, okay? But it's promising! I guess I'll find out at dinner." She caught the hint of concern in Molly's face, mixed with curiosity. "Look, I appreciate your advice, but can we drop it for now? I need some time to process everything."

"Fair enough," Molly conceded as she pulled up to the apartment building. "Goodnight, Jenny. Just remember, you deserve someone who treats you right."

"Thanks, Molly," Jenny murmured, giving her friend a small, grateful smile before stepping inside.

The door clicked shut behind her, sealing away the biting chill of the winter night. Jenny went upstairs and unlocked her door. She shrugged off her coat and hung it on the hook, the warmth of the room already seeping into her bones.

As she prepared her dinner, she let the rich tones of Upton Sinclair's *Boston* fill the room through her audiobook, immersing herself in the vivid descriptions of another time and place. The sizzling of the frying pan and the clatter of utensils provided a rhythmic accompaniment to the narration, grounding her in the present.

Jenny sat down at the small kitchen table, her simple meal steaming on the plate before her. She lost herself in the intricate tapestry of Sinclair's words, allowing the story to temporarily eclipse her own concerns and uncertainties.

As she scraped the last remnants of her dinner from the plate, Jenny pondered the upcoming evening with Sean. Would there be a spark between them? Could he be someone she could depend on and trust?

The soft hiss of water from the faucet filled the bathroom as Jenny cupped her hands to catch the stream, feeling its warmth against her skin. She splashed her face, rivulets tracing her cheeks before dripping onto the porcelain sink. With a sigh, she reached for her toothbrush, bristles springing back beneath the pressure of her fingers.

"Trust your instincts," she murmured to her reflection. "But be cautious."

As she scrubbed at her teeth, the taste of mint mingling with lingering flavors of her meal, Jenny's thoughts drifted to her upcoming dinner with Sean.

"Will you be able to win him over?" she asked herself silently, nudging aside the doubts that threatened to crowd her thoughts. The words remained unspoken, yet their weight hung heavy in the air.

Jenny rinsed her toothbrush under the faucet and set it

down, then cupped her hands once more to rinse her mouth. The water swirled and disappeared down the drain, carrying away the remnants of toothpaste and uncertainty alike.

"Only one way to find out," she whispered to her reflection, a wry smile playing at the corners of her lips.

She turned off the light, plunging the bathroom into darkness, and padded through the dimly lit apartment. Her feet sunk into the plush rug, and she relished the familiar sensation as she made her way to her bed.

With a final glance around the room, Jenny slipped beneath the covers, the sheets unfolding and welcoming her in. The darkness of the night enveloped her, and she allowed herself to drift into its embrace.

CHAPTER
TEN

THE FLUORESCENT LIGHTS overhead cast a sterile glow on the cramped office as rookie Agent James Hartley stood before his superior officer, feeling like a specimen under a microscope. Thorn regarded him coldly from behind his desk. His stern expression bore down on James, making it difficult for him to maintain eye contact.

"Agent Hartley," Thorn began, his tone sharp and unforgiving. "I'm growing concerned about your progress in this case. There's been no significant breakthrough."

James clenched his fists at his sides, struggling to keep his voice steady. "I'm doing everything I can, sir."

"Are you?" Agent Thorn interjected in disapproval. "Because from where I stand, it seems as though you've gotten a bit too . . . close to the subject."

"Every step I've taken in this investigation is purposeful," James insisted, his jaw tightening. "I'm gathering valuable intel—"

"Valuable intel?" Thorn cut in skeptically. "You've had

ample opportunity to find evidence of criminal activity, yet all you've reported are suspicions and hearsay."

"Winters is cautious," James said, struggling to keep his emotions in check. "I believe she's hiding something, but I need more time to uncover it. Just this morning she was searching how to get into a union, and we know she already has a union job. She may be trying to infiltrate legitimate labor organizations as part of her leftist plot."

"Time is not something we have in abundance, Agent Hartley," Thorn replied, his eyes narrowed.

"Sir, please," James pleaded desperately. "I can do this. I just need more time."

"Your time is running out," he warned. "I expect a significant breakthrough by next week, or I'll be forced to remove you from this case."

James felt the heat rise to his cheeks. "I assure you—"

"Enough, Agent Hartley," his boss cut him off, his tone icy. "We need results, not excuses. I expect an update on your findings by next week, and if there's no progress, I'll be forced to reassess your involvement in this case. Do I make myself clear?"

"Crystal," James replied through gritted teeth, suppressing the frustration boiling within him.

James fought to suppress the storm of emotions raging within him—frustration, fear, and an overwhelming sense of failure. His hands clenched into fists at his sides. He nodded curtly as he responded, "Understood, sir."

He turned on his heel and exited the office, his superior's disappointment heavy on his shoulders.

CHAPTER
ELEVEN

ON FRIDAY EVENING, Molly completed a full week of ferrying her friend to work and back. "Good thing I got laid off," she commented. "Who else would drive you around every day? This must be the slowest car repair in the Commonwealth of Massachusetts, and yet you're going out to dinner with the mechanic."

Jenny laughed. "I appreciate you, girl," she said. "Maybe you're right . . . why am I rewarding his behavior?"

Molly pulled her car up to Jenny's building. The two women sat in silence for a moment, before Molly placed a reassuring hand on Jenny's arm.

"Hey," she said, "This will be good for you, Jen. Just relax and enjoy yourself."

Jenny took a deep breath, attempting to steady her racing heart as she stepped out of the car. It was then that she noticed Sean, leaning casually against his own vehicle parked in front of her building. He looked dashing in a dark button-up shirt and well-fitted jeans, the sunlight catching in his brown hair and illuminating his handsome features.

"Hey, Jenny," Sean greeted warmly, his eyes locked on hers.

"Hi, Sean," she replied, managing a small smile. She could feel Molly's encouraging gaze on her back, willing her to take this leap of faith. She gestured back to her friend. "Sean, this is my friend Molly."

"Hey," Sean said, directing his attention toward the woman still seated in the driver's seat. "Nice to meet you. I'm Sean."

"Hey there, Sean," Molly replied with a friendly grin. "I've heard a lot about you." One eyebrow went up mischievously, making Jenny blush.

"Hopefully all good things," Sean said with a chuckle, and turned back to Jenny. "Shall we?"

"Almost," Jenny replied with a nod. "Just let me change out of my uniform and I'll be right back."

"Of course," Sean agreed with a smile. As Jenny turned to wave goodbye to Molly, her friend watched her go with a knowing smile.

In minutes, Jenny reappeared and met Sean at his SUV, her nerves beginning to dissipate as they made light conversation. When they arrived, Sean held the door open for Jenny, inviting her to enter the cozy Italian restaurant first. The dim lighting and soft music playing in the background immediately enveloped them, creating an atmosphere like a warm embrace on a cold winter's night. Jenny's expression flickered with appreciation as she glanced around the intimate space.

"Nice pick," she said.

"Thought you might like it," Sean replied nonchalantly, with a touch of relief.

A waiter led them to a table tucked away in a quiet corner. The white tablecloth was adorned with a single red candle, casting a gentle glow that seemed to soften the edges of reality. As they took their seats, the delicious smells wafting from the kitchen mingled with the sound of dishes clinking and laughter bubbling from other patrons.

"Smells amazing, doesn't it?" Jenny remarked, inhaling deeply as they perused the menu.

"Absolutely," Sean agreed, scanning the list of pasta dishes and hand-tossed pizzas.

As they each considered their options, the conversation between them flowed naturally. They spoke of books they'd read, places they'd visited, dreams they'd tucked away for safe-keeping. Through it all, the chemistry between them was palpable beneath the surface.

"Have you ever been to Italy?" Jenny asked.

"Once, a long time ago," Sean replied with a hint of nostalgia. "I'd love to go back someday."

"Maybe we should go together," Jenny suggested daringly.

"Maybe we should," Sean echoed, his gaze locking onto hers.

As the comforting aroma of garlic and tomatoes swirled through the air, Jenny found herself relaxing into the cushioned seat. The wood-paneled walls and dimly lit sconces cast a warm, intimate glow over the dining space, inviting her to open up in a way she hadn't expected.

"I've been reading this incredible Upton Sinclair novel lately," Jenny began hesitantly, tracing the edge of her wine glass with a delicate finger. "It's just . . . it's so powerful, you know?"

"Which one is it?" Sean asked, leaning slightly forward.

"It's called *Boston*," she replied, excitement bubbling within her. "It's about how the justice system is rigged in favor of the rich. The depictions of the living and working conditions of the working class and the poor really resonate with me. I struggle to make ends meet too . . . but, I mean, not like what people were dealing with in the 1920s."

"Tell me more about it," Sean encouraged, allowing his hand to rest close to hers on the table.

"You see," Jenny continued, growing more animated, "the characters are so real, and Sinclair doesn't shy away from exposing the harsh reality of the times. Reading it makes me feel . . . less alone, somehow. It makes you question everything you think you know about who are the good guys and who are the bad guys."

"Sounds like a fascinating read," Sean said, his gaze never leaving hers. "But what do you mean by struggling to make ends meet? What do you do for work?"

"Being an armored truck driver doesn't pay as well as you might think," Jenny sighed, her shoulders slumping a little. "I barely have enough to cover rent, let alone anything else. Sometimes, I can't help but dream of a different life—one where I'm not constantly worrying about how I'll survive another month."

"Jenny, I had no idea," Sean murmured, his fingers brushing against hers in comfort. "Is there anything I can do to help?"

"Thanks for offering, Sean," she smiled sadly. "But no, of course not. I just need to keep pushing forward and hope that things will get better eventually."

"Let me at least be here for you, Jenny," Sean suggested tentatively. "I know it's not much, but sometimes having someone to talk to can make all the difference."

"Thank you, Sean," Jenny whispered, her eyes shining with gratitude. "That means more to me than you can imagine."

As their fingers intertwined on the table, a sense of connection and understanding blossoming between them, it was clear that the seeds of something deeper had taken root.

Sean's gaze never left Jenny's face as she spoke, the candlelight casting a warm glow on her features. He nodded thoughtfully, his attention fully focused on her words and emotions, probing deeper into her thoughts.

"Are there any other authors you like?" Sean inquired gently, genuinely curious.

"Definitely," she responded, a small smile playing on her lips. "I love F. Scott Fitzgerald, Virginia Woolf, and James Baldwin, just to name a few."

As they delved further into their conversation, waiters moved discretely around them, placing plates of food before them. The creamy fettuccine Alfredo was a perfect blend of rich, velvety sauce and expertly cooked pasta, while the crisp Caesar salad was adorned with golden croutons and shavings of parmesan.

"Have you ever tried writing anything yourself?" Sean asked, twirling a forkful of fettuccine around his fork as he awaited her answer.

"Once or twice," Jenny admitted, tucking a strand of hair behind her ear. "But I'm not that good at it. I mostly write for myself—it helps me process the world around me."

"Maybe you could share your writing with me some time," Sean suggested with a hint of eagerness. "I'd be honored to read your work."

Jenny blushed slightly and looked down at her plate, her fingers playing with a stray crouton from her salad. "Maybe . . . maybe someday," she murmured.

"Whenever you're ready, Jenny," Sean assured her.

As they continued to eat, the conversation flowed effortlessly between them, touching on everything from music to politics, their bond growing stronger with each shared thought and laugh. The Italian restaurant had become their sanctuary, a place where they could reveal the most intimate parts of themselves without fear of judgment or rejection.

Finally, as the last morsels of food disappeared from their plates and the candles flickered low, it was clear that neither of them wanted the night to end.

"Thank you for tonight, Sean," Jenny whispered, her eyes shining with gratitude and affection. "You've made me feel like I'm not alone in this world."

"Believe me, Jenny," Sean replied sincerely, "the pleasure has been all mine."

With a contented sigh, Sean reached for the bill that had been discreetly left at the edge of the table. As he scanned the charges, his hand brushed against Jenny's, causing a shiver to run up her arm. She looked up at him with reluctant anticipation.

"Like I said, my treat," Sean said softly, his gaze holding hers. Jenny hesitated for a moment before giving a small nod and a smile of thanks. He paid the bill and helped her into her coat, the gentle press of his hands on her shoulders sending another thrill through her.

Outside, the city streets were awash in the golden glow of streetlights, casting long shadows on the pavement as they walked to Sean's car. The traffic hummed around them, seemingly in harmony with the sotto voce conversations taking place behind closed doors and under flickering signs.

Jenny stared out the car window as the familiar landmarks of her neighborhood slid by, their shapes softened and transformed by the shifting patterns of light and shadow. In the distance, she could see the dark outline of her apartment building looming against the night sky.

As they approached, the harsh glare of brake lights illuminated the narrow alley leading to the entrance, casting an eerie red glow over the cracked and stained concrete. Sean pulled up to the curb, shifting into park and turning off the engine. The sudden silence seemed to amplify the tension between them, filling the car with a palpable energy.

"Thank you for tonight," Jenny said. She reached for the door handle, but Sean's hand on her arm stopped her.

"Wait," he whispered, his eyes searching hers. "I just want to make sure you're okay."

"Of course I am," Jenny replied, her throat tightening around the words. "Why wouldn't I be?"

"Because we've opened up to each other tonight," Sean said gently, "and I know that can be scary. But I promise you, Jenny, whatever happens next, I'm here for you. And I'm not going anywhere."

With those words, something inside Jenny seemed to crumble and fall away, leaving her feeling exposed and vulnerable in a way she had never experienced before. As tears welled up, she knew that she could no longer deny the truth— she was falling for Sean, and there was no turning back.

"Thank you," she whispered, finally allowing herself to lean into the warmth of his embrace for just a moment before leaving the car.

The door to Jenny's apartment building loomed before them, its chipped paint and brass handle gleaming under the harsh glare of a single streetlight. The evening breeze had picked up, sending a scattering of leaves skittering across the pavement, as if in anticipation of their parting. "Let me walk you to your door," Sean said, not ready to leave her just yet.

"Thank you for dinner," Jenny said softly as they approached the front door. "And for listening." Her hands trembled as she fumbled with the brass handle and opened the door.

"Of course," Sean replied, his eyes never leaving hers. "It was my pleasure." He hesitated for a moment, then stepped closer. "I just want you to know that I'm here for you, Jenny. Whatever you need."

"Thank you," she whispered, her heart pounding so hard in her chest that it threatened to leap out of her throat. She could see the nervousness in his gaze, the way his fingers twitched at his sides as if he were fighting some internal battle.

"Jenny," Sean said softly. "Can I . . . may I kiss you goodnight?"

She didn't hesitate, didn't pull away. Instead, she simply nodded, her pulse hammering beneath the thin skin of her wrists.

His touch was tentative at first, unsure, but as their lips met, something seemed to ignite between them—a spark that quickly grew into an all-consuming flame. They leaned into each other, lost in the sensation, until the need for air forced them apart.

"Goodnight, Sean," Jenny murmured.

"Goodnight, Jenny," he replied, his eyes lingering on her face even as she slipped through the doorway and into the dimly lit corridor beyond.

The door clicked shut behind her, the sound echoing through the empty hallway like a gunshot. She leaned against it for a moment, her thoughts racing, before finally turning to make her way up the creaking staircase toward her apartment.

As she reached the first landing, she glanced back at the door, wondering if he was still there, watching her retreat. Her heart pounded in anticipation, a mixture of excitement and anxiety coursing through her veins. The accelerating rhythm of her pulse beat in syncopation with the soft creaks of the old building.

A few steps away, hidden in the shadows on the other side of the door, Sean's fingers grazed his lips, still tingling from the kiss. He exhaled, a quiet release of breath he'd been holding since their parting. His heart raced with a blend of exhilaration and nervousness, unsure of what the future held.

With one last lingering look at the door that separated them, Sean turned and descended the stairs. Outside, the wind continued to howl, tugging at his coat as he made his way back to his car. But despite the chill, there was warmth spreading through him. As he drove away into the night, his thoughts were consumed by her, replaying their conversation, their laughter, and the taste of her lips on his.

Max Thompson, leaning against the worn wallpaper of the dimly lit basement stairwell, peered through the crack of the slightly open door and the adjacent wall. His face fell as he watched the scene unfold before him—Sean's hesitant posture, Jenny's response, and their lips meeting in a brief, tender moment.

"Are you kidding me?" Max muttered under his breath, his hands clenching into fists. Max held his breath as Jenny started up the stairs. His heart pounded in his chest, a mix of anger and adrenaline coursing through him. As soon as enough time had gone by to avoid awakening suspicion, Max pushed himself off the wall and stalked upstairs toward Jenny's door.

"Hey there, neighbor," he said, forcing a smile as Jenny looked up in surprise. She recovered quickly, though, her expression shifting to one of guarded curiosity.

"Max, what are you doing here?" she asked, her tone cautious.

"Can't I just stop by to say hello?" he replied. "I saw you and your friend. He seems like a nice guy."

Jenny hesitated, her fingers tightening around the edge of the door. "Yeah, he is," she said finally, with a hint of defiance. "But that's really none of your business."

"Of course," Max said, his smile not quite reaching his eyes. "I just wanted to make sure everything's okay. I worry about you sometimes."

"Thanks, but I can take care of myself," Jenny snapped, irritation flashing across her face. She started to close the door, but Max wedged his foot in the gap, stopping it from shutting completely.

"Wait, Jenny," he pleaded, desperation seeping into his voice. "I just . . . I need to talk to you. Please."

"Fine," she sighed, relenting. "What do you want?"

Max swallowed hard, searching for the right words, the ones that would keep her from slipping through his fingers entirely. But failing to come up with a good story to explain himself, Max laughed it off. "Just kidding, neighbor," he said. "Have a good night."

"You too," Jenny replied, attempting to brush off the weird feeling this interaction had provoked in the pit of her stomach.

CHAPTER
TWELVE

MAX'S FINGERS danced over his phone screen as he texted Molly.

> Max: Have you heard from Jenny lately?

> Molly: Of course! Just saw her this morning. Why?

> Max: Just wondered. She's been acting kind of sketchy.

> Molly: ??!?

> Max: I'd keep an eye on that guy she went out with if I were you.

Molly couldn't shake the feeling that something was amiss. Her gut told her that Jenny was in danger, and she couldn't ignore it. The suspicion sent shivers down her spine.

Meanwhile, Sean texted Jenny.

> Sean: Hey, how's your day going?

Jenny: Good, thanks! What's up?

Sean: Just checking in. I noticed something odd with your car when I was fixing it. You didn't mention anything about an accident, did you?

Jenny hesitated before responding, her brow wrinkling in confusion. She racked her brain for any memory of an accident but came up empty.

Jenny: No, I haven't been in an accident. Why do you ask?

Sean: Oh, it's probably nothing. Just thought I'd double-check with you. Anyway, your car should be ready soon.

Jenny stared at the screen, a feeling of unease building within her. Shaking it off enough to get back to work, she slipped her phone back into her pocket. She stood at the back of the armored truck, scanning the rows of heavy canvas bags filled with cash. The weight of responsibility bore down on her as she checked and double-checked each bag against the manifest. One mistake could cost her not just her job, but also her precarious financial stability.

"Hey, Winters, you almost done?" Frank, her burly colleague, called from the cab. "We're running behind schedule."

"Almost," she replied, trying to hide her stress. In truth, the exhaustion was creeping up on her, settling into her bones like a fine layer of grime that no shower could wash away.

As Jenny secured the last bag, she caught a glimpse of her reflection in the truck's rearview mirror. Her short, straight hair was plastered to her forehead with sweat, and dark circles hung under her eyes. She looked every bit as worn down as she felt.

"Good to go," she finally said, slamming the door shut with more force than necessary.

"About time," Frank muttered, revving the engine impatiently.

As the truck pulled away from the curb, Jenny allowed herself a moment to lean against the cool metal, her body trembling with fatigue. She couldn't afford to lose this job. It was the only thing keeping her afloat in a sea of mounting bills and rent payments.

Meanwhile, back in Quincy, Molly sat in a cramped room with a dozen other participants, listening to a career center facilitator drone on about the importance of networking. She fidgeted in her seat, trying her best to look engaged, lest she anger the facilitator and lose credit for the workshop, jeopardizing her unemployment benefits.

"Remember, your network is your net worth," the facilitator said, flipping to the next slide in her PowerPoint presentation.

"Excuse me," Molly ventured, raising a hand. "But isn't that kind of an unrealistic expectation for people who are unemployed and struggling to make ends meet? I mean, networking events can be expensive."

"Great point, Ms. . . .?" the facilitator trailed off, waiting for Molly to provide her name.

"Brown," she replied.

"Ms. Brown," the facilitator continued with a condescending smile. "You'd be surprised at how many free or low-cost networking events there are if you just do some research. You have to invest in yourself if you want others to invest in you."

"Right," Molly said, biting back a retort. She couldn't afford to get on the facilitator's bad side, but it was infuriating to sit there and be talked down to as if she hadn't tried everything already. The workshops were a maze of patronizing advice and dehumanizing bureaucracy, but she had no choice but to play the game.

As the workshop wore on, it became increasingly difficult for Molly to maintain her composure. Each thinly veiled insult to her intelligence chipped away at her resolve until all she wanted to do was scream. But she reminded herself of Jenny—her friend who was struggling just as much, if not more, than she was. If Jenny could keep pushing forward, then so could she. She texted Jenny to say she was on her way to pick her up.

Relieved her shift was finally over, an exhausted Jenny climbed into Molly's car. She'd barely said hello when her phone rang. The screen lit up, displaying an unfamiliar number, but the area code was a 617, so she picked up.

"Hello?" she answered hesitantly, pressing the phone to her ear.

"Hey, Jenny. It's Sean—your car's all set. You can swing by anytime to pick it up."

"Oh, hi!" she replied, unable to contain her eagerness. "Thanks," she continued, trying to regain her dignity.

"Any chance you could make sure to pick it up while I'm here? I'd love to see you," Sean whispered conspiratorially.

"I'd love to," she whispered back. In a normal tone again, she asked, "How long will you be there?"

"I'll be here for another hour and a half," he replied. "Does that work?"

"It does. See you then," Jenny responded with a grin.

"Looking forward to it!"

Jenny stared at the phone for a moment after hanging up with a smile that was totally out of proportion to the news she'd just received, however anxious she actually was to get her car back. There was something about the way Sean spoke— intimate, yet playful; affectionate, yet not as if he had any claim over her. In short, he was intoxicating.

"What was that?" Molly asked, with one eyebrow raised. "You just win the lottery?"

Jenny laughed and shook her head.

"It was Sean. My car's ready."

"Damn, I've never seen anyone so happy to get their nasty old car back!" Molly laughed. "Want me to bring you to the shop instead of home, then?"

"Would you?" Jenny asked, gratitude filling her eyes. Molly nodded, bemused by her smitten friend.

"Of course."

As they drove in silence, Molly glanced sideways at Jenny —her usually unflappable demeanor had given way to the softness of a person with a serious crush.

After she pulled into the parking lot, Molly unfastened her seatbelt too. "Don't worry," she told Jenny jokingly. "I'll give you some alone time with your man. But I'm not passing up the opportunity to see if there's another hot mechanic in this shop for me."

Jenny laughed. "I'm pretty sure it's just Sean and Eddie, but it won't hurt to find out!"

As they approached the mechanic's shop, a figure stepped out from behind a battered pickup truck and into the flickering light. Eddie Hanson, the shop owner, was a burly man with sun-weathered skin and a gruff demeanor that belied his kind nature.

"Jenny," he said with concern. "I'm glad you're here. I wanted to talk to you about Sean."

His eyes darted around nervously as if he were afraid of being overheard. Jenny raised an eyebrow, searching his face for answers.

"What about him?" she asked cautiously.

Eddie hesitated, wringing his grease-stained hands together. "Look, I don't want to get involved in anything, but something doesn't feel right. Just be careful, okay? I'm not sure Sean is one of the good ones, if you know what I mean."

Molly, never one to miss an opportunity, sidled up to Eddie, her brown hair cascading across her shoulders as she tilted her head flirtatiously. "What about you, Eddie," she purred, tracing a finger along the rough stubble lining his jaw, "are you one of the good ones?"

His cheeks flushed a deep crimson. "I am," he said, pulling away from Molly's touch. "I'm such a good one that I'm a married man."

Molly tossed her head back and smiled. "Your loss!"

But Eddie's gaze remained steady on Jenny, the weight of his warning hanging heavy in the air. "Just be careful around Sean," Eddie stammered. "Trust your instincts."

"Thanks for your concern, Eddie," Jenny said composedly. "But I've been taking care of myself for a long time now. I know a bad one when I see one. Now where can I find my car?"

Eddie shook his head in defeat and pointed her to the back.

As they walked toward the workshop where Jenny's car awaited, Molly couldn't shake the feeling that they were being watched. The hairs on the back of her neck stood on end, and she found herself glancing over her shoulder as if expecting to see a sinister figure lurking in the shadows.

The workshop was a cavernous space, its high ceilings and vast floor area filled with the scent of oil and metal. Pools of light from overhead lamps illuminated the sleek lines of cars in various states of disrepair. Molly looked quickly around the dimly lit room until she saw a figure emerge from the gloom—Sean, wiping his grease-stained hands on a rag, his face betraying his eagerness to see Jenny and perhaps a touch of disappointment that Molly was in tow.

"Your car's all set, Jenny," he said, his tone as smooth and cold as the steel tools that glinted on the walls behind him. "I think you'll find I've done my absolute best for you." He grinned.

"Thanks, Sean," Jenny mumbled, suddenly shy, unable to meet his steady gaze. In spite of herself, Eddie's warning had left her a little shaken.

"Let me walk you to your car," Sean offered, his tone almost nervous, as he tried to read Jenny's mood.

Molly took the hint. "Looks like you're all set, Jenny?"

"Yes, thanks so much for the ride, Molly."

The two friends hugged goodbye, and Molly headed back to her car.

Having regained his confidence, Sean rested his hand on the small of Jenny's back. "It's just out here, in the side lot," he said, handing Jenny her car keys and leading her to the exit. She leaned into his touch and walked with him, moving ever so slightly closer as she did.

As they stepped outside, the cool night air enveloped them, providing a temporary reprieve from the oppressive atmosphere of the workshop. They reached Jenny's old Accord and she unlocked the driver's side door. She could sense Sean moving closer, though he was behind her. When she turned back around, he wrapped his left arm around her hips and cupped the back of her neck with his right hand. "Seems like it's time to say goodnight again," he murmured as he drew her face up to meet his, and they melted into a long kiss.

Still holding her close, he said softly, "I'm sorry my shift isn't over for another hour. I wish I could take you out."

"Me too," Jenny breathed in reply. "Call me," she said coyly and disentangled herself, though it was the last thing she wanted to do. Her heart racing, she stepped into her car. Sean stepped away, slow and confident, with a radiant smile glowing in his eyes, and watched until she pulled out of the parking lot before re-entering the shop.

CHAPTER
THIRTEEN

MOLLY WAS UNEASY. In spite of her flippant reaction to Eddie's warning, she kept replaying the moment in her head. Eddie had unequivocally indicated that he wasn't interested in either of them with his comment about being a married man. So he wasn't jealous; he wasn't trying to warn Jenny away from Sean to have a chance with her himself.

Molly couldn't quite put her finger on what was wrong. She thought back on everything Jenny had told her about Sean. She had met him at the mechanic's shop. If Eddie thought he was a bad apple, why did he let Sean work there? Sean had gone to Jenny's apartment to pick her up for dinner. But as far as Molly knew, Jenny didn't know where Sean lived, or who he might live with.

Out of an abundance of caution, she decided to do a little surveillance and see what she could find out. If Sean was into something criminal, it would be better for Jenny to know upfront. Molly moved her car down the street within view of the shop, parked, and cut the lights.

She sat in her beat-up sedan, the faint scent of cigarette

smoke lingering from years past. She looked intently back and forth between Eddie's mechanic shop and the rearview mirror, checking for any sign of movement. She drummed her fingers on the steering wheel, a restless energy pulsing through her.

"Come on, come on," she muttered under her breath, tapping her foot impatiently. In about ten minutes, she saw Jenny pull out of the parking lot, alone in her car. So far so good.

Five minutes later, the front door of the shop creaked open, and Eddie stepped out with Sean close behind him, talking animatedly about something Molly couldn't hear. She squinted, trying to make out their expressions, but the distance made it impossible.

Eddie appeared agitated over something, but Sean was the opposite, waving his hand lazily before slipping into his SUV parked near the shop.

As Sean pulled away from the curb and passed her, Molly started her engine, the rumble of the old beast echoing down the street. She followed Sean at a discreet distance, her suspicions growing. She couldn't shake the feeling that something was off.

"Where are you going, Sean?" she whispered to herself, gripping the steering wheel tighter. The buildings gave way to glass storefronts and crowded sidewalks. People streamed in and out of restaurants and bars, the air thick with laughter and music. An old church stood sentinel on one corner, its spire cutting through the darkening sky, while the parking garage loomed ahead.

Molly watched keenly as Sean drove into the Kilroy Square garage in Quincy Center. Her pulse quickened at the sight of it, the antiseptic fluorescent lights creating a sinister atmosphere. She followed him in, her tires echoing through the empty space as she maneuvered past pillars and parked cars.

"Could he live in one of the new condos? On a mechanic's wages?" Molly wondered, her mind racing with possibilities. The shadows seemed to stretch out from the corners, reaching for her car. She could feel the weight of her suspicions growing heavier, pressing down on her chest as she continued deeper into the garage.

"Keep your cool, Molly," she muttered, forcing herself to take a deep, calming breath. Her hands were clammy on the steering wheel, and she wiped them on her jeans before adjusting her grip.

Sean's SUV turned a corner, disappearing from her line of sight for a moment, and Molly sped up to keep him in view. The concrete walls closed in around her, amplifying every sound—the hum of her engine, the squeak of her brakes, and the steady drip of water from the ceiling.

"Come on, Sean, where are you going?" she whispered once more, scanning the rows of parked cars for any sign of movement or life. As she rounded the corner, she caught a glimpse of his car, tucked away in a dark corner of the garage. Her heart caught in her throat.

The shadows of the parking garage seemed to deepen, drawing Molly's gaze to Sean's SUV as it pulled up alongside a nondescript sedan. Her breath caught in her throat, heart pounding against her ribcage, as she observed the clandestine meeting from her vantage point.

"Who the hell is that?" she muttered, squinting to make out the figure emerging from the other vehicle. The man was tall, his bulky frame shrouded in a long overcoat. He glanced around furtively before approaching Sean, who stepped out of his own car with a guarded expression.

Whispers of conversation drifted on the stale air of the garage, the words indiscernible yet laden with tension. Molly strained her ears, desperate to catch even a fragment of their exchange. But it was the man's gloved hand, slipping a small package into Sean's palm, that sent a shiver down her spine.

"Shit," she breathed, feeling the weight of her discovery settle upon her. What had she stumbled upon? Was Sean involved in something dangerous—or worse, illegal? She swallowed hard, her fingers tightening on the steering wheel as she considered her options. Confront him? Call the police? Neither seemed like the right course of action, not without more information to go on.

Lost in her turbulent thoughts, Molly forgot the most basic rule of operating a vehicle: always check your surroundings before moving. With adrenaline coursing through her veins and her mind racing, she shifted the car into reverse and hastily backed up, eyes still trained on the unfolding scene before her.

"Damn it!" she cursed as the rear bumper collided with a garbage can, the metallic clang echoing through the garage. Panic surged through her as both Sean and his mysterious contact turned toward the sound.

Molly's chest constricted, her heart pounding wildly as the gravity of her mistake sunk in. There was no time to waste; she had to get out of there before they realized who she was. Her thoughts raced, attempting to calculate her next move.

"Get a grip, Molly," she muttered under her breath, willing herself to stay focused. The men were still watching, their bodies tense and poised for action. If she didn't do something soon, she knew they'd come looking for the source of the noise—and that could only end badly for her.

She forced herself to breathe deeply, trying to steady her

trembling hands on the wheel. With a final glance at the two men, she put the car into drive and slowly pulled away from the scene, wincing at the sound of the garbage can scraping against the pavement. She felt their eyes on her, but she refused to meet their gaze. Instead, she focused on navigating through the garage, her heart lodged in her throat as she prayed they wouldn't follow.

As she exited the parking structure and merged onto the narrow street, she allowed herself a moment to exhale. Temporary relief washed over her, but she knew it wouldn't last long. The questions swirling in her mind refused to abate: What was Sean involved in? And how far was she willing to go to find out the truth?

The glare of the streetlights bounced off the wet pavement as Molly's grip tightened on the steering wheel. She glanced in the rearview mirror, catching a glimpse of Sean's SUV pulling out of the parking garage. The tension that had momentarily dissipated roared back to life, coiling around her.

"Damn it," she muttered under her breath, glancing between the road ahead and the mirror, gauging the distance between them. Sean's vehicle inched closer, its headlights casting eerie patterns on the streets. She noted the way he held a radio to his mouth, his lips moving with an urgency that set her nerves on edge.

"Come on, Molly, think," she whispered, her voice barely audible above the hum of the engine. A cold sweat trickled down her spine, sending shivers racing through her body. She knew she couldn't outrun him for long—not in this old clunker of a car. But she had to try.

Her foot slammed down on the gas pedal, propelling the car forward with a jolt. Sean's vehicle swerved behind her, keeping pace as if they were locked together by some unseen force. She could almost feel the weight of his gaze burning into her, threatening to consume her whole.

"Leave me alone!" she cried out, though the words were lost in the roar of the engines and the pounding of her heart. Desperation clawed at her throat, choking her until it felt as if she couldn't breathe. Each turn she made in an attempt to lose him only seemed to bring him closer, their cars weaving through the dark streets like predator and prey locked in a deadly dance.

"Is this really happening?" she thought, terror threatening to swallow her whole. "What does he want from me?"

In the distance, Molly spotted the entrance to a narrow alley—too narrow for Sean's SUV to follow. It was a gamble, but she had no other choice. She veered into the alley, sending a spray of water flying as her tires screeched against the pavement. The walls closed in around her, suffocating her with their oppressive weight.

"Please," she prayed as she navigated the tight space. The engine roared beneath her, its fury echoing her own as they hurtled toward an uncertain future.

Sean's SUV skidded to a halt at the alley's entrance, unable to continue the chase. His eyes narrowed as he watched the taillights disappear, his grip tightening on the radio. A string of muttered curses filled the air, each one more venomous than the last.

"Lost her . . ." he hissed into the radio, the words dripping with frustration and rage. "But not for long."

As Molly emerged from the alley, her breaths ragged and uneven, she knew that the danger was far from over. Her heart slammed against her ribcage, each beat threatening to break free from its bony confines. She sped through the dark streets of Quincy, the city lights blurring into a kaleidoscope of colors in her peripheral vision. Her hands clenched around the wheel, her leg muscles tense, she cast furtive glances in the rearview mirror, searching for any sign of Sean's pursuit.

The wail of sirens shattered the night's tense silence. Molly's stomach twisted into knots as she glimpsed the flashing blue lights in the mirror. Two police cruisers pulled up behind her, one on either side, boxing her in as they slowed to a stop.

"Damn," she muttered under her breath, her eyes darting between the officers and the road ahead. She knew she couldn't outrun them—but at least Sean couldn't hurt her while she was talking to cops. With a resigned sigh, she eased her foot off the accelerator, guiding the car to the curb.

"License and registration, ma'am," the officer on her left demanded, his tone stern and unwavering. He was a tall man, broad-shouldered and square-jawed, with a dusting of salt-and-pepper stubble across his cheeks. His partner stood back, arms crossed, studying Molly carefully.

"Of course, officer," Molly replied, her voice trembling despite her best efforts to maintain composure. She reached for her purse, rummaging through its contents until she found the requested documents. As she handed them over, she caught a glimpse of the other cruiser—a pair of fresh-faced rookies watching from its interior, their gazes shifting between her and their seasoned colleagues.

"Ma'am, I'm going to need you to step out of the vehicle," the officer said, his tone betraying a hint of sympathy. It was clear he'd seen cases like hers before—people who got caught in the wrong place at the wrong time, their lives irrevocably altered in an instant.

Molly hesitated for a moment, her mind racing with anxiety and doubt. She knew that once she stepped out of the car, there would be no going back—no escaping the consequences of her actions. But what choice did she have? The officers were simply doing their job.

"Alright," she whispered, unclipping her seatbelt and opening the door. As she stood, she felt the weight of her situation settle over her shoulders, pressing down on her. She glanced back at the officer, her face pleading silently for understanding, for mercy.

He looked away, his expression unreadable.

"Don't move," he instructed her. "My partner will run your license."

For what seemed like an eternity, Molly stood with her hands on the roof of her car. Finally, the second officer re-emerged from his cruiser.

"Ma'am, we're placing you under arrest," the second officer informed her icily. "We received a request from ICE to detain you as a possible undocumented alien." He moved to handcuff her, the metallic click echoing through the night.

"Wait . . . please," Molly stammered, her face pale and stricken. "There's been a mistake. I—I'm an American citizen."

"Save it for the judge," the officer replied coldly, cutting off her protestations. "You won't be the first undocumented Irishwoman trying to pass yourself off as an American in Quincy. You have the right to remain silent. Anything you say can and will be used against you in a court of law . . ."

As the Miranda rights droned on, Molly's thoughts spun in dizzying circles. How could this be happening? Was this all a result of her digging into Sean's suspicious behavior? Could he have somehow set her up?

FOURTEEN

MOLLY SWALLOWED HARD, fighting back tears as the handcuffs tightened around her wrists. The future loomed ahead, cloaked in shadows and uncertainty—and Molly Brown had never felt more alone.

The immigration detention center loomed before her like an imposing fortress, its gray walls a stark contrast to the blue sky above. Molly was escorted inside by two officers, their faces impassive and unreadable. The world outside—the swaying trees, the distant sounds of traffic—seemed to recede into oblivion as the heavy door slammed shut behind her.

"Welcome to your new home," one of the officers muttered sarcastically.

Molly glanced nervously around the sterile, institutional interior. Fluorescent lights buzzed overhead, casting a harsh glare on linoleum floors and rows of metal benches. Women clad in orange jumpsuits shuffled past, their expressions somber, resigned.

"Name?" barked a matronly woman behind a thick glass window, snapping Molly out of her daze.

"Uh, M-Molly Brown," she stammered.

"Brown . . . Molly . . ." the woman muttered, rifling through a stack of papers. "Here you are. Another undocumented alien, huh?"

"I'm a US citizen," Molly insisted. "I was born at MGH."

"Right." The woman smirked, but there was no warmth in her eyes. "Of course you were." With a dismissive wave, she motioned for the guards to lead Molly away.

"Take her to cell block D," the woman instructed. "And make sure she understands our rules: no talking, no personal items, and absolutely no contact with the outside world. Got it?"

"Understood," replied one of the officers, nudging Molly forward.

As they walked down the narrow corridor, Molly's heart pounded in her chest. Her mind raced, searching for some explanation, some semblance of logic amid the chaos that had engulfed her life. Was it really just a coincidence that she'd stumbled upon Sean's mysterious rendezvous, only to find herself trapped in this cold, unforgiving place?

"Here we are," announced the officer, stopping in front of a heavy steel door. "Cell block D."

He swung it open to reveal a cramped room lined with bunk beds, each adorned with a thin, lumpy mattress and a threadbare blanket. The air was damp and stale, tainted by the scent of despair. Molly's fellow detainees huddled in corners, their eyes hollow and listless.

"Find an empty bunk and keep your mouth shut," the officer instructed, shoving her inside. "You'll have plenty of time to think about what you've done."

With that, the door slammed shut with an echoing clang.

Molly scanned the room, her heart aching at the sight of

the other detainees—mothers, daughters, grandmothers—all separated from their loved ones, their lives indefinitely on hold. She could hear the faint sound of muffled sobs, the stifled whispers of prayers for deliverance.

She found an empty bunk and sat down, the flimsy mattress sagging beneath her weight. Around her, the oppressive silence weighed heavily, broken only by the occasional shuffle of feet or rustle of fabric. There would be no sympathetic ear to listen to her fears, no comforting words to soothe her frayed nerves. In this place, she was truly alone.

The sun had long since surrendered to the night, casting a cold pallor over the detention center. Molly lay on her bunk, staring up at the cracked ceiling tiles, the frigid air seeping through her thin cotton shirt. The echoes of muted conversations and stifled sobs floated around her like ghosts.

In this place, all the rights she usually assumed a detained person would have were unavailable to her. Some authority somewhere had decided that her right to be in the United States was in question. But she'd never even left the US. She had no passport from anywhere. The whole mess could be cleared up with a call to her mother to ask her to bring Molly's birth certificate to whoever needed to see it, but the officers wouldn't allow her to communicate with the outside world.

As the night stretched on, the vise of the absurdity and impossibility of her situation wrapped itself around her heart, threatening to choke out what little hope remained.

CHAPTER
FIFTEEN

THE BULLPEN of the FBI office hummed with an electric undercurrent, a palpable energy that buzzed through the air. Agents hurried through the maze of cubicles, their polished shoes squeaking on the linoleum floor. The scent of freshly brewed coffee mingled with the faint tang of dry erase markers, as whiteboards covered in hastily scribbled notes dotted the open space. Amidst the orchestrated chaos stood Agent James Hartley, his tall frame obscured by the tangle of desks and computer screens. He absentmindedly ran a hand through his hair, eyes darting from one corner of the room to another, attempting to gauge the source of the excitement.

"Lauren's done it," announced a fellow agent proudly as he slapped James on the back. "Brought in the arms dealer."

"Bernard?" James asked, arching an eyebrow in surprise. The mention of Lauren Bernard's name elicited a mixture of admiration and rivalry within him. The two had been pitted against each other since their first day at the Academy, and the competition for a promotion had heightened the tension between them.

"Yep, she's got him locked up," the agent replied, grinning broadly. "She's on her way up. Get ready to celebrate."

As if on cue, the doors to the bullpen swung open and in strode Lauren, her dark skin glowing with triumph. A confident smile played on her lips as she entered, and the room erupted into applause. Agents crowded around her, offering hearty congratulations and firm handshakes. She beamed, her white teeth gleaming against her smooth complexion.

James watched the scene unfold from a distance, trying to quell the knot of envy tightening in his chest. It wasn't just the accolades; it was the satisfaction of seeing a case closed, justice served. As much as he longed for that sense of accomplishment, his own investigation of Jenny weighed heavily on his conscience.

"Nice job, Bernard!" an agent called out, clapping Lauren on the shoulder. "That was one hell of a takedown!" Her face lit up with pride, her eyes sparkling.

"Thanks," she replied. "It's been a long time coming."

"Excellent work," another added with a pat on the back.

Lauren Bernard reveled in the praise she was receiving. A mixture of pride and satisfaction emanated from her as she recounted the story of how she had managed to arrest the notorious arms dealer they'd been tracking for months. Her smile, unwavering and contagious, spread throughout the squad.

"Tell us again how you got him," one agent urged.

"Alright, alright," Lauren replied, feigning modesty. "So, I noticed something off about the shipment schedule, right? That led me to dig deeper, and I found a pattern. That's when I knew we had him."

The agents leaned in, captivated by her every word. James Hartley leaned against his cubicle, watching the celebration from afar. He noted the way Lauren basked in the attention, her posture straight and confident. As fellow rookie agents, he and Lauren had always been in competition, pushing each other to be better. But today, her accomplishment felt like an unattainable benchmark.

"Congratulations, Lauren," Hartley finally managed, extending a hand as he waded through the throng of agents. She grasped it firmly, her grip strong and unyielding.

"Thanks, James," she replied, gleaming with pride. "You're not far behind. I know you'll crack your case soon."

"Let's hope so," he muttered, releasing her hand and taking a step back. "Guess this puts you in the lead for that promotion, huh?"

"Maybe," Lauren said, grinning. "But don't count yourself out just yet."

"That's one thing I'd never do," James replied with a wry smile.

"Good," Lauren said, leaning against his desk, her eyes locked onto his. "We need more agents like us, making a difference."

"Right," James agreed, feeling the pressure mount within him. His gaze slid over to the stack of files on his desk, Jenny's name peeking out from beneath the pile.

"Whatever it takes, right?" Lauren asked with a hint of challenge.

"Absolutely," he responded, his voice barely more than a whisper. He could almost taste the bitter tang of deceit on his tongue.

"Remember," Lauren said, her tone softening, "we're on the same side."

"Of course," he echoed, his pulse quickening. In that moment, James felt the weight of responsibility pressing down upon him; the scales of justice tipped precariously in the balance.

There was a part of him that longed for the neat, decisive simplicity of Lauren's victory, the straightforward satisfaction of bringing a criminal to justice. But his own investigation was anything but simple, the lines between right and wrong blurred beyond recognition.

James glanced around the room, taking in the faces of his fellow agents as they reveled in their shared triumph. How easy it would be, he thought, to bring Jenny down, to notch another win for the FBI. But the cost of that victory weighed heavily on his mind.

Lauren patted him on the shoulder before moving back to the crowd, leaving James to wrestle with the tempest of emotions that threatened to consume him. As he glanced around the bullpen, he registered the buzz of activity and the electric hum of camaraderie. He was part of a team that lived and breathed by the oath they'd taken together, yet he felt alone in his struggle.

"Another win for the good guys, huh?" a nearby agent remarked, clinking his coffee mug against Lauren's in a toast.

As Lauren moved on to accept more congratulations, James took a slow breath, trying to steady himself. The cacophony of agents laughing and sharing stories echoed through the bullpen, amplifying the tension that coiled in his chest. He glanced at his watch, then fidgeted with his tie, as if the pressure of the fabric against his throat was too much to bear.

James closed his eyes briefly, attempting to quell the storm of emotions raging within. When he opened them, he was met with the file on his desk, Jenny's name staring back at him like an accusation. The choice between duty and desire loomed before him, its grip tightening with each passing moment.

"Whatever it takes," he whispered to himself.

James leaned against his desk, tracing the edge of his coffee mug with one finger as he observed the celebration from a distance. His knuckles whitened with the effort it took to hold back his inner turmoil, yet the agents around him seemed oblivious to the storm raging within him.

"Remember when we took down that smuggling ring a few months back?" an older agent reminisced, leaning back in his chair and gesturing expansively. "Now that was a wild ride!"

"Absolutely!" his younger partner concurred, wide-eyed with awe. "But this case, this one's going to be hard to top."

"Indeed," the elder agent agreed, raising his cup in salute.

"Remember that time when Lauren single-handedly took down that perp twice her size?" another agent recounted, eliciting a chorus of laughter and exclamations of awe.

"Oh yes," Lauren chimed in, her expression one of pride and amusement, "he never saw me coming."

"Hey, James," another agent called out, "you've got some big shoes to fill now, buddy. Better step up your game!"

The remark was meant in jest, but it struck a chord deep within James, who felt an icy shiver run down his spine. He forced a weak smile and nodded, his mind already racing with thoughts of Jenny and the impossible decision that lay before him.

"Sure thing," he replied, the words hollow and strained, betraying the weight of his conflicted emotions.

"Hey, James!" Lauren called out, beckoning him over with a jubilant wave of her champagne flute. "Come and tell us about your latest lead on Jenny!"

The room seemed to shrink as the words hung heavy in the

air, James's heart thundering in his ears as he gritted his teeth in frustration. A knot tightened in his stomach, bile rising like a bitter tide.

"Sure thing," he replied tersely, forcing a smile onto his face as he approached the throng of agents. They parted before him like the Red Sea, their eyes alight with curiosity and anticipation as they turned to listen to his tale. But as he opened his mouth to speak, the words caught in his throat as he tried to force them out into the open.

"Actually, I've got to . . . uh, take this call," he stammered, gesturing vaguely toward his silent phone. Without waiting for a response, he pivoted on his heel and strode purposefully toward the bullpen door.

"Whatever it takes," he repeated to himself, the phrase now a desperate mantra. The room swirled before him, a blur of faces and voices that only served to heighten his sense of isolation. And then, without warning, he felt something snap within him.

"Excuse me," he muttered, shoving past the other agents who looked on in surprise. His steps quickened, fueled by a newfound urgency, until he was all but sprinting toward the exit.

The door slammed shut behind him with a resounding crash, the force of it reverberating through the hallway as James strode away from the celebration—and from the expectations that threatened to consume him.

"Agent Hartley," a man called from behind, causing James to halt in his tracks. He turned to find Agent Miller approaching, his expression one of concern. "Is everything alright?"

"Fine, just . . . need some air," James stammered. But even as he uttered the words, he knew they rang hollow. His mind was a whirlwind of questions and doubts, and the need for answers gnawed at him.

"Big day for Lauren, huh?" Agent Miller said, trying to lighten the mood. "We're making progress, James. Your time will come."

"Right." James forced a smile, but it felt more like a grimace. "I'll catch up with you later, Miller." He pivoted away, resuming his march down the hallway. In the wake of his departure, the laughter and applause dwindled, replaced by a palpable tension that clung to the air like a heavy fog. And as James paused at the elevator, taking a deep, steadying breath before pressing the button, he knew that there could be no turning back.

CHAPTER
SIXTEEN

JENNY'S FINGERS drummed against the kitchen counter, the tick-tock rhythm echoing through the small apartment. Her gaze flitted between the stovetop clock and her phone, waiting for a response from Molly. She hadn't heard from her in a while, and it was unlike Molly to not text back.

A sudden gust of wind slipped through a crack in the window, stirring up the papers scattered across the worn wooden table. Jenny watched as an unopened envelope danced through the air before it settled on the floor by her feet. It was a peculiar sight, as if the universe itself had conspired to hand-deliver her misery.

She picked up the envelope, her fingers tracing the return address. Internal Revenue Service. Trepidation clenched her stomach, and she hesitated for a moment, knowing that its contents could only spell more bad news.

With a resigned sigh, Jenny tore open the letter, her hands shaking ever so slightly. As she unfolded the crisp paper, her eyes fell upon the exact amount owed: $8,513. A chill crawled down her spine, freezing her heart in place. It wasn't just the number that frightened her, but the words that followed, threatening to take the debt out of her paycheck. Her already dicey financial situation had just become a nightmare.

"Damn it," she muttered under her breath, crumpling the letter into a ball and tossing it onto the table. She turned back to her phone, her hope of talking everything through with Molly fading fast. She couldn't bear the thought of her mother, Ellen, finding out about the IRS notice. It would be yet another burden Jenny didn't have the right to impose on her.

"Come on, Molly," she whispered, willing her phone to light up with a response. "I need you. You always know what to do."

But the screen remained black, and Jenny's heart grew heavier by the second. She picked up the crumpled letter, smoothing it out between her hands. The words seemed to mock her, their ominous message a stark reminder of how quickly life could spiral out of control.

"Eight thousand dollars," she murmured, letting the reality of the number sink in. It was more than she'd ever imagined owing, and the thought of her paycheck being seized sent a shudder through her body.

Jenny hesitated, her thumb hovering over Sean's number on her phone screen. The thought of reaching out to him for support felt like an admission of defeat, but the weight of her situation was too heavy to bear alone.

"Hey, it's Jenny," she said when he answered, her voice shaking despite her best efforts to sound composed. "I just . . . I could really use someone to talk to. Are you free?"

"Of course," Sean replied. "You sound upset. Do you want me to come over?"

"Could you? I know it's a lot to ask, but I just don't want to be alone right now."

"Give me fifteen minutes. I'll bring wine and takeout."

"Thank you, Sean," she whispered, relief momentarily stemming the tide of panic that threatened to engulf her.

As she waited, the apartment seemed to close in around her. She paced the room, feeling as though she were navigating a treacherous labyrinth—one wrong turn, and the walls would swallow her whole.

When the doorbell finally rang, Jenny nearly stumbled over her own feet in her haste to let Sean in. He stood in the doorway, tall and strong, with deep eyes that seemed to see far more than they should. In his hands, he carried a bag of fragrant Thai food and a bottle of red wine.

"Hey," he said softly, stepping inside and enveloping her in a warm embrace. "I'm here."

"Thanks," she managed, her voice muffled against his chest. "It's just been a really rough day."

"Let's eat, and you can tell me all about it," he suggested, guiding her to the couch.

They settled into the cushions, plates balanced on their laps and glasses of wine in hand. The heady scent of curry mingled with the earthy aroma of the wine. As they ate and sipped, Jenny found herself confiding in Sean more than she ever thought she would.

"Everything feels like it's falling apart," she admitted, staring into the depths of her nearly empty glass. "I don't know how much more I can take."

"Hey," Sean said gently, laying one hand on her shoulder and refilling her wine glass with the other. "You're stronger than you think, Jenny. You'll get through this, whatever it takes. I'll be here for you every step of the way."

His promise hung in the air between them, a beacon of hope in the encroaching darkness. And as the night wore on,

Jenny found herself leaning into the warmth of his presence, seeking solace in the connection that seemed to grow stronger with every passing moment.

The raindrops slid down the windowpane, casting a distorted sheen over Jenny's face as she sat nestled in the old threadbare couch. Her eyes shimmered with unshed tears. Sean watched her from the corner of his eye, noting the almost imperceptible tremble in her hands as she clutched the wine glass.

"So what happened?" he asked softly.

"Sean," Jenny whispered, "I'm drowning in debt." She shook her head slowly, as if to cast off a heavy burden. "I owe thousands of dollars to the IRS, and they're threatening to take it straight out of my paycheck."

His heart caught in his throat. He steeled himself, reminding himself of his purpose for being there. "Jenny, I . . . I think there might be a solution," he began cautiously, trying to gauge her reaction through the dim light of the room.

"What do you mean?" Her eyes locked onto his, searching for some kind of hope in his words.

Sean took a slow sip of his wine, buying time to carefully choose his next words. "You drive around with huge sums of money every day, right? Money that could change your life if you had access to even a small fraction of it." He paused, letting the implication hang heavy in the air between them.

"Are you saying . . ." Jenny hesitated, "that I should steal from the bank?"

"Look," he said quietly, leaning toward her, "I don't want you to think I'm encouraging you to do anything illegal, but maybe you deserve a break. Maybe you deserve some help—more than those banks ever needed, and you know they get bailouts whenever they ask. It's just an option to consider."

The silence that followed seemed to stretch on for miles. Sean held his breath, waiting for the storm of emotions that would no doubt be swirling through Jenny's mind.

"Sean, I appreciate your concern," she murmured finally, "but . . . I can't do that."

"Jenny," Sean said earnestly, reaching out to take her trembling hand in his own, "you don't have to decide right now. Just think about it. You deserve a chance at a better life, and I'm here to help you however I can."

As their fingers intertwined, he felt the warmth of her touch, the way her pulse quickened beneath his fingertips. He wondered if she could feel the same tension within him.

"Thank you, Sean." The words were little more than a sigh, but they carried with them an emotion that threatened to engulf them both—a growing bond forged in shared secrets and whispered confessions.

"Would you mind staying?" Jenny asked softly, searching Sean's face for any hint of hesitation. "I could use the company."

"Of course," he replied, a gentle smile touching his lips. "I wouldn't want you to be alone right now."

As Sean settled back into the couch, Jenny dimmed the harsh overhead light, allowing the apartment to be enveloped in a soft, comforting glow. The low hum of the refrigerator mingled with the rhythm of the rain outside, creating a soothing soundtrack to the evening. She lit a vanilla-scented candle, letting its warm fragrance permeate the air, and joined Sean on the couch.

The atmosphere seemed to shift around them, as if the very walls of Jenny's apartment were drawing them closer together. Shadows danced across their faces, casting their features in an intimate chiaroscuro that belied the tension still lingering between them. And yet, despite the undeniable connection that was forming, both struggled to find the words to fill the silence.

For a moment, they simply sat there, side by side, lost in the weight of everything left unsaid. It was only when Sean turned toward Jenny, his hand reaching out to tuck a stray strand of hair behind her ear, that she felt her resolve begin to crumble. There was something inexplicably tender about that simple touch—an unspoken promise that he would do whatever it took to keep her safe.

"Thank you, Sean," she whispered, her voice catching in her throat as she fought to hold back tears. "I don't know what I would have done without you tonight."

"Jenny," he murmured, his thumb brushing away a tear that had escaped its confines, "you don't need to thank me. I'm here for you, no matter what."

As they settled into the embrace of the couch, the barriers between them seemed to dissolve, replaced by a sense of trust and understanding that went beyond words. They leaned into one another, finding comfort in the warmth of their shared embrace. Jenny's eyes felt heavy, her body sinking into the cushions as she leaned against Sean's strong shoulder. His steady breaths were a comforting metronome, lulling her into a sense of security she hadn't felt in ages.

"Hey," Sean whispered. "Are you tired?"

"Yeah," Jenny admitted, nestling closer to him. "But I don't want this night to end."

"Who says it has to?" he replied, the corner of his mouth lifting in a tender smile. He rose from the couch and offered his hand to her, leading her through the moonlit apartment to the sanctuary of her bedroom.

They climbed into bed, navigating the delicate dance of

tangled limbs and shared warmth. The intimacy of their close-ness seeped into every pore, an intoxicating elixir of comfort and desire. As Jenny's head came to rest on Sean's chest, listening to the steady thrum of his heartbeat, a feeling of contentment settled over her.

"Thank you," she murmured, her words a feather-light caress against his skin. "For everything."

"Always," he promised, his arms encircling her in a protective embrace.

Yet, as they drifted toward the welcoming arms of sleep, Sean's thoughts were a whirlpool of conflict and doubt. The sound of Jenny's breathing, so soft and steady against his chest, was a bittersweet reminder of what he was—and what he had to do.

CHAPTER
SEVENTEEN

MAX THOMPSON MADE his way up the stairs of the apartment building the next morning. His body tensed as he recognized the silhouette of Sean retreating from Jenny's door.

In that moment, Max recalled the warning he'd given Jenny—a warning that seemed to fall on deaf ears. He couldn't shake the feeling that something was off about Sean. There was a darkness lurking behind those calculating eyes, and it gnawed at him with each passing day.

"Morning, neighbor," Jenny greeted him as she opened her door. Her hair was disheveled, her cheeks tinged with glowing pink.

"Morning," Max replied, trying to mask his feelings. "Thought you might need some caffeine." He held out a steaming cup of coffee, freshly brewed and black as night.

"Thanks," she said, taking the cup from his hand. The warmth spread through her fingers, a fleeting sensation of comfort amidst the chaos of her life.

"Listen, Jenny . . . I saw Sean leaving just now." Max hesitated, unsure how to express his fears without sounding overbearing. "I know I've told you this before, but I really don't trust that guy. Just . . . be careful, okay?"

Jenny let out a small laugh, dismissing his concern with a wave of her hand. "Honestly, Max, you worry too much. Sean's alright," Jenny said with a tight-lipped smile. "Did you want to come in?"

"Yeah, there was one other thing I wanted to talk about— Molly." Max stepped into her apartment as Jenny opened the door wider for him. The morning sunlight filtered through the blinds, casting a warm glow across Jenny's living room floor.

"Have you heard anything from her?" Max asked, his fingers tapping nervously on the edge of his cup.

Jenny shook her head, her face clouded with concern. "Not a word. It's been days now . . . I'm starting to get really worried."

Max mirrored her expression, his hair falling into his face as he looked down at the floor. "Yeah, me too. She's not one to just disappear like that."

"Maybe we should call the police," Jenny suggested quietly. The thought of their friend in harm's way sent a chill down her spine.

"Let's give it another day or two," Max replied, trying to sound more optimistic than he felt. "She might just be laying low for a bit."

After an awkward pause, Jenny broke the silence. "Thanks for the coffee, Max. I'd love to hang out, but I have to get ready for work."

"Of course, of course," he replied, standing and shoving his hands into his pockets. Jenny walked him to the door, and Max pulled her into a fumbling hug that Jenny wriggled out of.

"Catch you later, neighbor," she said lightly.

"Yeah, see you later," he replied, his eyes on the floor.

Jenny shut the door gently behind him and went back to the couch. She hadn't entertained Sean's idea to rob her own truck for a moment, but the next option she'd come up with hardly felt any more ethical than a heist.

Jenny reached for her phone, her fingers hesitating over the screen before dialing a familiar number. The line rang once, twice, before a tired voice answered.

"Hello?"

"Hey, Mom," Jenny said, forcing a brightness into her tone that didn't reach her expression. "I know you have to get to work, so I'll cut right to the chase. I got a letter from the IRS . . . It's not good."

"Jenny, what did you do?" Ellen's tone was sharp, tinted with disappointment—a reaction Jenny had come to expect over the years.

"I didn't do anything wrong, Mom. There's just some mix-up with my taxes," she insisted, swallowing the lump in her throat. "I was wondering if . . . maybe you could help me out, just this once?"

A heavy sigh crackled through the phone, the sound carrying with it the weight of past arguments and unspoken frustration. "I wish I could, baby, but I've got my own bills to pay. You know how it is."

"Of course," Jenny said quickly as she choked back tears. "I understand. Thanks anyway, Mom."

"Good luck, sweetheart," Ellen replied, the line going dead a moment later.

Jenny stared at the phone in her hand, the cold weight of rejection settling in her chest. She longed for the days when her mother's embrace would chase away the darkness, but those times were long gone.

With the weight of her money trouble and concern for

Molly heavy on her shoulders, Jenny stepped out of her apartment into the cold morning air. Her breath formed clouds of mist around her as she walked to her car. The frost on the windshield served as a cruel reminder of the chill that had infiltrated her life recently.

She drove to work in silence, her thoughts racing faster than the engine's hum. As she pulled into the facility parking lot, the imposing yet nondescript brick building loomed before her like a prison. This was where she spent her days, locked in a cycle of hardship and disrespect.

"Morning, Jenny," Frank called as she entered the building. "You look like you could use some coffee."

"Thanks, Frank, but I've already had my fill," she replied tersely, trying to brush past him.

"Aw, c'mon, don't be like that," he said, blocking her path. "I'm just trying to be friendly."

"Your 'friendly' is suffocating. Now, if you'll excuse me, I have a job to do." She didn't bother hiding her irritation as she stepped around him, her jaw clenched tight.

"Fine, fine," he muttered, his gaze following her as she made her way to the locker room. "Just trying to help."

Jenny ignored him, shaking her head as she changed into her uniform.

Despite the disrespect that seemed to follow her like a shadow, Jenny forced herself to focus on her tasks. But as the day wore on, the challenges piled up, and Jenny felt herself sinking deeper into despair. She longed for a lifeline, something to pull her back from the edge, but it seemed as though the world was determined to test her strength.

As Jenny steered the armored truck through the congested streets of Boston, each stop brought a new challenge, a fresh opportunity for her to be reminded of her place in the world.

She pulled up to the first location, a small convenience store tucked away in a narrow alley. The owner, a rotund man with a thick mustache, hardly looked up from his newspaper as she approached.

"Here for the pickup," Jenny announced, her voice steady despite the tight knot in her stomach.

"About time," he grumbled, his eyes never leaving the page. "You people are always late."

Jenny clenched her jaw as she hefted the heavy bags of cash into the truck. She didn't bother correcting him—that they were actually ahead of schedule. What was the point? It wouldn't change anything. Instead, she focused on the rhythmic thud of the bags hitting the metal floor, the way the truck trembled ever so slightly beneath her feet.

She moved on to the next stop, a seedy bar with neon lights flickering in its windows, casting an eerie glow on the damp pavement below. She could hear the raucous laughter and clinking of glasses even before she entered, the smell of stale beer and sweaty day drinkers assaulting her nostrils. When she finally emerged with the bar's earnings, a group of patrons jeered from their seats around the pool table.

"Hey sweetheart, need a hand with that?" one asked, his tone dripping with condescension.

"Or maybe a foot rub after your long, hard day?" another chimed in, smirking.

Jenny gritted her teeth and ignored them, her grip tightening around the canvas straps. Inside, her thoughts churned, but outwardly, she refused to give them the satisfaction of seeing her falter.

By the time she reached her final pickup, a small grocery store with a cracked sign hanging precariously above the entrance, her patience was wearing thin. She could feel the weight of the day pressing down on her shoulders, heavy and insistent.

"Are you sure you can handle all that?" the cashier asked skeptically, eyeing the bags she'd just loaded onto the dolly. "You're not exactly what I'd call 'burly.'"

"Trust me," Jenny replied, her voice strained and brittle. "I've got it."

As she wheeled the money out to the truck, she felt a wave of frustration wash over her. All day, she'd been met with sneers and jibes, and for what? Just so she could scrape by, barely keeping her head above water?

She slammed the doors shut behind her. The world felt cold and unyielding, indifferent to her struggles, and as she climbed into the driver's seat, she wondered if it would ever get any easier.

CHAPTER
EIGHTEEN

AS JENNY STEPPED out of her truck at the end of her shift, her phone buzzed with a new text message. It was Sean, asking if there was any chance he could take her out for a beer that evening. A thrill ran through Jenny—she hadn't expected to hear from him so soon after their first night together. Trying not to sound too eager, she typed back an affirmative response and suggested a pub near her apartment building. Sean asked when he could pick her up, and Jenny responded that Boston traffic was wild as usual, but she would text him when she got home. He replied with a thumbs-up emoji, which made her smile.

The rain fell in a relentless drizzle that evening, dampening Sean's hoodie as he held the door open for Jenny. She hurried into the pub, her coat pulled tight around her petite frame, and the warmth of the dimly lit room enveloped them both. The pub was a cozy refuge from the weather outside; dark wood-paneled walls, adorned with photographs of past residents, absorbed the laughter of the patrons huddled around small round tables.

"Thanks," Jenny said, shaking out her wet hair, her eyes meeting Sean's for a moment before she walked toward the bar. Her every step exuded a quiet confidence, born of years spent navigating a world that seemed to challenge her at every turn.

Sean followed, setting his backpack down at the booth Jenny chose. "What are you having?" he asked. "Looks like they have Sam Adams, Blue Moon, Harpoon, and Bud Light on tap."

"A pint of Sam would be great, thank you," Jenny replied. She watched him order two pints of beer at the bar, remembering their intimacy the last time she saw him.

"Here you go." Sean handed Jenny a pint, his fingers briefly brushing against hers. "I love the vibe of this place. You're lucky to have it right around the corner."

"Cheers to that," Jenny replied, raising her glass. As they sipped their drinks and exchanged stories about their day, Jenny was drawn in by Sean's charm. He was so different from anyone else she'd met—a shade of mystery enveloped him, making him all the more intriguing. She found herself wanting to know more about him.

Despite the comfortable atmosphere, an undercurrent of anticipation simmered between them, the memory of last night lingering. The evening progressed, punctuated by laughter and flirtatious glances, as the pub's patrons around them became increasingly blurry background figures. The smell of worn leather and aged wood mingled with the scent of hoppy lager, creating an atmosphere both comforting and mysterious. In their cozy corner booth, it felt as though time had slowed down, allowing them to indulge in each other's company without the weight of the outside world pressing in.

"Okay, so just for fun," Sean began, his voice low and

conspiratorial, "let's say you were going to plan a heist on your own truck. How would you do it? What tools would you need?"

Jenny looked at him, her eyes shining with mischief. "Are you asking me to incriminate myself?" she teased, her lips curving into a sly smile.

"Come on, it's all hypothetical," Sean replied with a wink. "I just want to see how that clever mind of yours works. I bet you could get five years' pay out of that thing in one night."

"Alright," she conceded, reaching for a napkin and pen from the small wooden caddy on their table. "But if anything goes missing, I'll know who to blame." She flashed him a coy grin.

Together, they hunched over the napkin, their heads nearly touching as they brainstormed ideas. Jenny started by listing the basic necessities: gloves, radios, and some sort of distraction to keep the other guards occupied. As Sean listened attentively, he added his own suggestions, such as a jammer for any security cameras and a police scanner to keep tabs on any potential response.

"I'd need to create a diversion," she mused aloud, as Sean watched her intently. "Something that would draw attention away from the truck without raising suspicion."

"Like a fire alarm?" he offered as he tried to keep up with her rapid-fire train of thought.

"Too obvious," she dismissed, shaking her head. "Maybe a staged car accident nearby, or a power outage. Something just chaotic enough to distract people without getting the cops involved too quickly."

"Okay, so once you've got your diversion, how do you get inside the truck?" Sean asked.

"Easy," Jenny replied, grinning mischievously. "I've got the keys, remember?"

"Right, of course," he stammered.

Jenny's plan unfurled like a map of her own making, each detail a testament to her resourcefulness and imagination. She spoke of utilizing decoys to confuse the authorities and creating diversions to buy time. The route she would take was a labyrinth of side streets and alleyways, far from the prying eyes of surveillance cameras. Her knowledge of the city's underbelly was uncanny, as if she had spent years studying its every nook and cranny.

"Once we've reached the rendezvous point, I'd have a team waiting with another truck," she explained, making the note on the napkin. "We'd transfer the cargo quickly and efficiently, leaving no trace behind."

"Another truck?" Sean asked, eyebrows raised in surprise. "That's bold."

"Bold, but necessary," she responded, a mischievous glint in her eye. "See, the original truck would be rigged with a GPS tracker. It'd lead the police on a wild goose chase while we made our escape."

"Wow," he breathed, impressed despite himself. "You really thought this through."

"Like I said, it's just a game," she reiterated with a shrug, seemingly unaware of the weight her words carried.

"Next, I drive the loaded truck to a predetermined location where my accomplices would be waiting," she explained with excitement. "They'd help me unload the cargo and transfer it to another vehicle—maybe a carpenter's van or something inconspicuous like that."

"Sounds like you've thought about this before," Sean

remarked, attempting to keep his tone light as he grappled with his conflicting emotions.

"Please," Jenny scoffed, waving away the suggestion. "I'm just making this up as I go along. It's all in good fun, right?" She glanced at him expectantly, searching for reassurance.

"Right," he agreed with a small smile that didn't reach his eyes.

"Anyway," Jenny continued, her enthusiasm undimmed, "once the cargo is secured, we'd split up and lay low until the heat died down. Then we'd make off with the spoils."

"Sounds like a solid plan," Sean murmured as he watched her animated features. "But let's hope you never have to put it into action, huh?"

"Of course not," she agreed, laughing lightly as she crumpled up the napkin and tossed it onto the table. "Like I said, it's just a game."

"Right," Sean echoed, projecting above the din of the bar.

As they continued to discuss their hypothetical heist, their laughter grew louder and more frequent. Each idea spurred another, more outlandish than the last, until they had concocted a plan worthy of a Hollywood blockbuster. Sean found himself captivated by Jenny's quick wit and resourcefulness, while she reveled in the fact that he seemed genuinely interested in her thoughts, her passions, and her dreams. As the hours slipped by, it became increasingly clear that their connection went far beyond the playful banter of their heist planning. There was an undeniable chemistry between them, simmering slowly beneath the surface of their shared laughter and mischief.

It was well into late evening when they finally decided to call it a night, both reluctant to part ways.

"Let me walk you home," Sean offered, his tone gentle yet

insistent as they stepped out into the crisp night air, the street-lights casting pools of golden light upon the pavement.

"Thank you," Jenny replied, smiling shyly as they began to navigate the familiar streets of her neighborhood. The air between them felt charged with anticipation, each stolen glance and brush of their fingertips sending a shiver down her spine.

As they approached an intersection, Sean noticed a car approaching at a speed that made him uneasy. Seizing the opportunity to protect Jenny, he reached out and grasped her hand, pulling her closer to him.

"Careful," he murmured, the warmth of his breath on her ear sending a jolt of electricity through her body. "That car doesn't look like it's going to stop."

"Thanks," she replied softly, her heart pounding in her chest as she felt the comforting weight of his hand move from hers to rest gently on her hip for the remainder of their journey home.

The night seemed to hold its breath as they walked together, the soft glow of the streetlights following Sean and Jenny as they approached her apartment building. For a moment, time seemed to stand still, suspended in the air.

"Thanks for tonight, Sean," Jenny said as she turned to face him. "I had a great time."

"Me too," he replied, his eyes locked onto hers, as if searching for a hidden meaning within their vibrant green depths. Slowly, he leaned in, his lips meeting hers in a tender, passionate kiss that sent waves of warmth radiating through her body.

When they finally broke apart, the intensity of their connection lingered in the space between them. Sean hesitated, his hand resting on the doorknob, a silent question hanging in the air. It was Jenny who answered it, reaching out to touch his arm gently, an invitation shining in her face.

"Would you like to come in?" she asked.

"Are you sure?" Sean responded, searching her face for any sign of doubt or hesitation.

"Positive," she said, her smile both inviting and vulnerable, as she opened the door and led him inside.

As they entered her cozy apartment, the muted light from the streetlamps outside cast a warm glow over the room, illuminating the threadbare couch and the scattered remnants of Jenny's day. They continued their conversation from earlier, the playful banter and shared stories weaving together, each thread drawing them closer and revealing more of their inner selves. As they spoke, Jenny found herself leaning in closer to Sean, her body instinctively seeking the warmth of his presence.

"Your heist plan was brilliant," Sean said. "I never knew you had such a devious side."

"Neither did I until tonight," she admitted, a mischievous smile playing on her lips. "It's funny how things can bring out hidden parts of ourselves, isn't it?"

"Definitely," he agreed, his gaze hungry as it lingered on her face.

The air felt charged with possibility, as if anything could happen in this suspended moment before reality came crashing back in. Slowly, almost hesitantly, their bodies began to gravitate toward one another. The space between them dwindled, as if guided by some magnetic force that neither could resist. Jenny's heart pounded in her chest, her pulse thundering in her ears as she leaned in, her gaze locked on Sean's.

His breath was warm against her skin, and she felt herself

shiver in response. They surrendered to the undeniable pull that drew them together, their lips and bodies meeting in a tenderness formed of secrets and desires left unspoken. As they melted into each other's arms, the world outside seemed to fade away, leaving them suspended in a bubble of time and space all their own.

CHAPTER
NINETEEN

THE MORNING SUN cast a warm glow over the imposing facade of the FBI building, while a soft breeze carried the scent of fresh coffee from a nearby street vendor. Agent James Hartley's heart hammered against his chest as he approached the entrance, the weight of the information he held heavy on his mind.

As he stepped through the revolving glass doors, the familiar hum of the fluorescent lights above him seemed to echo his unspoken anxiety. He strode through the sterile hallways, feeling like an imposter in his own skin, the sensation amplified by the contrast between his tattooed exterior and the pristine surroundings of the bureau.

After what felt like an eternity, he arrived at the door to Henry Thorn's office. James hesitated for a moment, steeling himself for the conversation that lay ahead. With a shaky hand, he raised his knuckles and rapped sharply on the wooden surface.

"Come in," came the gruff response from behind the closed

door, and James felt a knot tighten in his stomach. It was clear that his superior was not in the mood for pleasantries.

As he pushed the door open, the sight of Thorn's office greeted him—a stark room devoid of warmth, its furnishings purely functional and impersonal. The only hint of personality was a single photograph of Thorn and his family, all bearing the same stern expression as their patriarch.

Thorn sifted through the stack of papers on his desk, his fingers drumming against the polished wood with a steady rhythm. The fluorescent light above cast stark shadows on his face, accentuating the lines etched by years of service. He sat behind his desk, fingers interlaced as he looked up at James with a steely gaze, his buzz cut emphasizing the hardness of his features. "Agent Hartley, what can I do for you?" he asked coldly.

"Before we discuss my case," James began, struggling to find the right words, "I wanted to apologize for my behavior at Lauren's party." He swallowed hard, feeling the weight of Thorn's gaze upon him. "My attitude was unprofessional, and I understand if it has caused some strain between us."

A faint flicker of acknowledgement crossed Thorn's stern features, but he remained silent, waiting for James to continue.

"I just wanted to clear the air," James added, trying to gauge Thorn's reaction, though the man's stoic facade revealed little. "That being said, I have some important information regarding the Winters woman and her recent activities that I think you'll want to see. The leftist."

With a nod, Thorn set aside the papers and directed his full attention to James. "Go on," he urged, his articulation clipped and precise.

James hesitated, swallowing hard. He could feel the weight of the words pressing down on him, as if they were physically heavy, their sharp edges cutting into his conscience. And yet, he knew he would do whatever it took to notch this win. Thorn's office seemed to shrink around them, the walls closing in like a vise as James delivered his findings.

"She . . . she has a plan," James stammered. "A detailed plan for a heist. It's clever, unexpected . . . and it involves her own truck."

"Go on," his superior urged, his curiosity evident.

"From what I've gathered," James continued, "she's been in contact with some unsavory characters who have expressed interest in the contents of her vehicle. It seems they're orchestrating a plan to make it look like an external job."

Thorn shifted in his seat, the leather groaning beneath him. His fingertips drummed against the desk, a staccato rhythm that echoed in the tight confines of the room. "Do you have proof of these allegations?" he asked. The question betrayed an undercurrent of doubt.

"Jenny's been meeting with some unusual associates from the criminal underworld," he said carefully, "at clandestine locations. Some of the conversations I overheard suggested that they were hatching a plan to intercept her truck and make off with its cargo."

As James relayed the details of Jenny's plan, he found himself caught in a whirlwind of emotions: admiration for her ingenuity and sorrow for the circumstances that had driven her to such desperation.

James unzipped the leather satchel, his fingers trembling ever so slightly as they reached for the envelope inside. The fluorescent lights of Thorn's office flickered overhead, casting distorted shadows across the room that seemed to dance with every beat of James's heart.

"Here," he said, offering the envelope to Thorn. "I have

photographs, documents, and transcripts of conversations implicating Ms. Winters in the planned theft."

Thorn accepted the envelope with a critical eye, his hands deftly extracting the contents. He rifled through the stack of photographs first, each one a captured moment of clandestine meetings and furtive exchanges. The images painted a picture that was both damning and undeniably real.

Next, he turned to the transcripts, scanning the lines with an intensity that betrayed his skepticism. The words on the page seemed to come alive under his scrutiny, forming a narrative that intertwined Jenny with a criminal underworld she had no place in.

"Surveillance reports?" Thorn asked, not looking up from the documents.

"Alongside the transcripts, yes. They corroborate the information I've provided." James tried to keep his voice steady, the weight of his actions bearing down on him.

The silence hung heavy in the air, punctuated only by the rustle of paper as Thorn continued to examine the evidence. As the minutes ticked by, James felt the tension coiling within him, tighter and tighter until it threatened to snap.

Thorn studied James for a beat, his gaze unyielding. The silence stretched between them, taut and brittle. Then, with a curt nod, he conceded. "Your investigation has been thorough, Agent Hartley," Thorn finally said, clearly impressed. "This is solid work. It appears we have a genuine threat on our hands."

"Thank you, sir," James replied. Relief washed over him in a cool wave, though it left a residue of unease in its wake.

"Ensure that everything is secured in the evidence room," Thorn instructed. "We will proceed with the necessary actions to intercept this theft and bring those responsible to justice."

James nodded, his mind racing with a thousand unspoken

thoughts as he took the envelope back from Thorn. The evidence within it felt heavier now, each item an irrefutable link in the chain that bound Jenny to her fate.

"Time is of the essence, Agent Hartley," Thorn said, his voice steel wrapped in velvet. "We must act swiftly to thwart their plans." He had leaned forward over the polished surface of his desk, hands clasped together, eyes alight with purpose.

"Of course, sir," James replied, feeling a cold knot tighten in his stomach. The weight of responsibility settled on his broad shoulders.

"Good. I'll get started on obtaining warrants and putting our team together." Thorn moved with precision, each movement calculated and efficient as he reached for the phone. His fingers danced across the buttons, summoning the resources he needed with the ease of long practice.

James stood at the edge of the room, watching the flurry of activity unfold before him. He was an observer, no longer the architect of this plan but a bystander to its execution. It felt strange, being so removed from the process, yet he knew it was necessary. Jenny's fate hinged on the delicate balance they maintained between truth and deception.

Thorn's voice cut through the air, terse and commanding as he spoke to subordinates. "I need search warrants expedited, and I need our best people assembled for this operation."

The office seemed to shrink around them, the shadows growing deeper and more oppressive as Thorn continued to issue orders. James felt the walls closing in, the air thickening until it was difficult to breathe. He knew what would come next—the raid, the arrest, the inevitable fallout—and it left him feeling hollow, as if a part of him had been scooped out and discarded.

"James," Thorn said, "you need to keep an eye on Winters.

Don't let her out of your sight. We'll be ready to move in as soon as the warrants come through."

"Understood, sir," James replied, feeling the weight of responsibility press down upon him. But he knew that Thorn trusted him to carry out this task, and that trust was not something he took lightly.

"Good," Thorn nodded. "And remember, discretion is paramount. No one can know what we're planning." The sternness in Thorn's expression left no room for doubt.

"Of course, sir."

"Stay close to the subject, but don't arouse suspicion," Thorn continued, his gaze pinned on James. "We can't afford any slip-ups now."

"Understood," James repeated, his heart pounding in his chest like a caged bird desperate for escape. He felt the enormity of the task before him, and with it, the crushing pressure to perform flawlessly.

"Agent Hartley," Thorn said, drawing James's attention back to the present. There was a rare glimmer of approval in the older man's face, a tacit acknowledgment that James's work had brought them to this moment. "You've done well."

"Thank you, sir," James murmured, unable to meet Thorn's gaze for fear that his own eyes would betray the profound unease within him.

"Dismissed," Thorn said, cutting through the tension that hung between them. James gave a terse nod and turned on his heel to leave the office, his footsteps echoing hollowly in the quiet space.

As James stepped out of the office and into the hallway, he couldn't shake the feeling that he was leaving something important behind. The corridor stretched before him, an endless expanse of cold linoleum and sterile walls that seemed to mirror the emptiness inside him.

He wondered if this was what victory always felt like.

CHAPTER
TWENTY

THE POUNDING on Jenny's door reverberated through the apartment complex, a relentless intrusion that shattered the early morning silence. A man's voice barked sharply, "FBI! Open up! Come out with your hands up!" The tension in the air was palpable, a living thing growing stronger with each word.

Max, startled awake by the commotion, stumbled out of his bed, his heart racing. He went upstairs and cracked the stairwell door open just enough to peer around the corner, watching as dark-suited agents swarmed around Jenny's door. His bloodshot eyes widened; behind the scruff and unkempt hair, concern etched itself into his features. Despite the haze from last night's indulgence still clouding his thoughts, he couldn't shake off the sense of terror and helplessness.

"Jenny," he whispered, guilt gnawing at him for not having done more to protect her. He felt powerless, like a ship caught in a tempest—tossed about and unable to navigate the treacherous waters. But there was no time for self-pity. He needed to act.

"Please, just open the door," he murmured, willing her with every fiber of his being. He knew her too well—her stubbornness and skepticism were part of her charm. In this situation, however, they could prove disastrous. If only she would comply, perhaps there was a chance things wouldn't escalate further.

"Last warning, Winters! Open up or we'll break it down!" the agent shouted.

"Damn it, Jenny," Max breathed, his chest constricting with anxiety. He clenched his fists, helpless and frustrated. This wasn't how it was supposed to be. They were neighbors, friends even. He'd wished they could be more.

"Please," he implored as the reality of Jenny's imminent arrest bore down on him. In this moment, the weight of his unspoken feelings for her threatened to suffocate him. He had to find a way to help her—whatever the cost to himself.

Jenny's eyes fluttered open, the pounding noise infiltrating her dreams and dragging her back to reality. Her heart raced in her chest as she struggled to make sense of the situation, her mind still foggy from sleep. She blinked, trying to clear the haze, and slowly sat up in bed.

"One of the neighbors must be into something," she whispered to herself, rubbing her temples with delicate fingers. The dim light of her alarm clock cast a faint glow across her room, allowing her to see the scattered clothes and books that formed a disorganized landscape around her. Jenny sighed heavily, feeling the weight of her exhaustion settle on her shoulders.

"Again?" Max muttered under his breath as the pounding continued, louder and more insistent this time. A cold sweat broke out on his forehead, his hands trembling slightly as he clenched them into fists. His heart thundered in his chest, a cacophony of fear and uncertainty that threatened to drown out everything else. He swallowed hard, his throat painfully dry, and tried to steady his breathing.

"Open up!" the FBI agent barked, his voice sharp and unforgiving. "Now!"

"Jesus, what is going on?" Jenny mumbled, the worry finally creeping into the edges of her thoughts that the door they were banging on might be hers. She slid her legs over the side of the bed, feeling the cold hardwood floor against her bare feet. Her hand reached for the edge of her nightstand, fingers brushing against the smooth surface of her phone.

"Jenny, please," Max whispered in panic. He could feel the tension radiating off the officers outside her door—the way they shifted their weight from foot to foot, their fingers hovering over their holstered guns.

"Last warning!" The agent's shout tore through the air like a gunshot, and Max flinched instinctively, his eyes widening with terror. "Open up or we'll break it down!"

"Damn it," Jenny breathed, her pulse quickening as she stumbled to her feet. The noise was no longer just an annoyance; it had become an immediate threat.

The crash of splintering wood and the violent thud of metal against the doorframe tore through the air. Jenny's heart leapt into her throat as she instinctively stumbled back, her legs trembling beneath her.

"Federal agents! On the ground!" A chorus of shouts filled the room with an overwhelming cacophony of authority and menace. Flashlights cut through the darkness, obliterating the soft, hazy glow of the moonlight filtering in through the curtains.

"Jesus Christ!" Jenny shrieked, her hands flying up to shield her eyes from the blinding light. The chill of the night air licked at her exposed skin, the thin fabric of her pajamas offering little protection against the sudden intrusion of cold reality. "What the hell is going on?"

"Jenny Winters, you're under arrest for conspiracy to commit robbery," one of the agents barked as he reached out to grip her arm with a gloved hand. The contact was like ice, jolting her nerves and sending a shockwave rippling through her entire body.

"Robbery? That's insane! I haven't done anything!" She screamed as fear and disbelief warred within her. Her mind raced, desperate to find some anchor to cling to amidst the storm of panic that threatened to consume her. But there was nothing—only the hollow echo of her own futile denial.

"Looks like we're adding resisting arrest," another agent growled, grabbing her other arm and wrenching her off balance. Together, they began to drag her toward the open doorway, her bare feet skittering helplessly over the hardwood floor.

"Please," she whispered, the word barely audible above the chaos that surrounded her. It was a plea that went unanswered, swallowed by the relentless march of justice.

"Please," she repeated as tears burned at the corners of her eyes. The agents continued to drag her out of her apartment, their grip unyielding and indifferent to her pain. They stepped over the battered threshold, severing Jenny's last connection to the life she had known.

The night swallowed her whole, and Jenny Winters disappeared into the abyss.

Max stood in his apartment, fingers trembling as he fumbled with his phone. In the darkness of the early morning hours, the screen's glow illuminated the frantic desperation etched across his face. He scrolled through his contacts, searching for Jenny's mother's number.

"Come on, come on," he muttered to himself, his heart pounding against his chest. But as he searched further, reality tightened its grip around him; he didn't have her number. A shudder of helplessness coursed through him, leaving him feeling even more powerless than before. It was as if he was trying to catch the wind in his bare hands, every attempt slipping through his fingers.

"Damn it," he whispered, clenching his fists. He couldn't give up now, not when Jenny needed him most. With renewed determination, Max tapped Molly's name in his contact list and raised the phone to his ear. The ring tone echoed in his ears, an anxious metronome counting down the seconds until the call connected.

"Pick up, Molly. Please pick up," Max pleaded, each unanswered ring gnawing at the edges of his already frayed nerves. Each unanswered call felt like a nail hammered into the coffin of his hope. He hung up, only to try again, his desperation mounting with every moment that passed.

"Max Thompson," he thought, "you're the last person who should be handling this." But there was no one else. No one else who knew Jenny and knew what had just happened to her.

"Jesus, Molly," Max muttered, running a hand through his unkempt hair. "Where the hell are you? I need you."

He tried calling her again and again.

"Please," Max whispered. "Please, Molly."

His phone pressed against his ear, Max felt as if the world

itself was holding its breath, waiting for the faintest sound of Molly's voice to pierce the darkness that surrounded him. But as the seconds ticked by, the silence grew heavier, more oppressive, threatening to smother him beneath its cold, claustrophobic embrace.

"Jenny," he thought, his heart twisting painfully at the memory of her tear-streaked face. "I'm so sorry."

A sudden vibration shook Max from his despair, the shrill tone of his phone slicing through the silence. Heart pounding, he snatched it up and saw Molly's name flash across the screen.

"Max," she said, her words rushing out, "I got your messages. What's going on?"

"It's Jenny," he choked out, clutching the phone as if it were a lifeline. "The FBI arrested her."

"Jesus," Molly breathed, the gravity of the situation evident in her hushed exclamation. "I'll be right over."

"Thanks, Molly. I didn't know who else to call."

"Of course," she replied resolutely. "Just sit tight."

The line went dead, leaving Max once again cloaked in silence. The foreign stillness of Jenny's apartment seemed almost sinister now, each shadow cast by the early morning light a reminder of her absence.

When Molly arrived, her face was pinched with worry, her light-brown hair disheveled as if she'd rushed out without so much as glancing in a mirror. She strode into Max's living room, vibrating with barely contained energy.

"Start from the beginning," she demanded.

Max recounted the events that had unfolded just hours before—the pounding on Jenny's door, the agents storming into her apartment, the look of utter disbelief etched upon her tear-streaked face as they dragged her away.

"Conspiracy to commit robbery?" Molly echoed incredulously when Max revealed the charge. "That doesn't make any sense. She's never been involved in anything like that."

"Exactly," Max agreed. "And now she's just . . . gone. Like she's been swallowed up by this nightmare, and I can't do a damn thing to help her."

Molly's eyes softened as she regarded him, her gaze searching his face for answers that neither of them possessed. "You're not alone in this, Max. We're both here for Jenny, and we'll do whatever it takes to get her back."

"Thank you," he whispered through a ragged breath. "I can't bear the thought of losing her."

"Neither can I," Molly admitted. "She means more to me than anyone else."

"Wait a second," Max burst out. "Where the hell have you been? Jenny and I have been trying to reach you all week."

A clouded moonlight filtered through the half-drawn curtains, casting a pale glow upon Molly's face as she sank into an armchair. "I would have said you wouldn't believe what happened to me, but after what happened to Jenny, I imagine you will."

"What?" Max asked, disbelief etched on his face.

"Yep." She sighed, her gaze distant. "Kind of a long story, but I followed Sean the night Jenny picked up her car. He was involved in some kind of suspicious exchange in a parking garage. I made a stupid mistake, and he caught sight of me, and next thing I knew, I was in a high-speed chase. I lost him but got pulled over for speeding by QPD. There was some crazy mix-up, and they thought I was an undocumented immigrant and sent me to detention. They wouldn't let me call anyone."

"Jesus . . ." Max murmured, his stomach knotting at the thought of Molly being subjected to such injustice.

"Then around five in the morning today an officer came to the cell and just said I was free to go," she continued bitterly. "No explanation given. And certainly no apology. So I went home and went to sleep; I figured I'd call you guys at a more normal hour. I thought the whole thing was just another example of my wicked bad luck, but the cops releasing me at the same time they were arresting Jenny cannot be a fucking coincidence, right?"

"Something's not right," Max observed, his jaw set in determination. "It's like they're trying to keep us all in the dark, confused and powerless."

"Exactly," Molly agreed, her hair falling across her face as she nodded. "And we can't let them get away with it. We need to find out what's going on, for Jenny's sake."

Max watched as she pulled out her phone, her slim fingers tapping against the screen with practiced ease. "Who are you calling?" he asked.

"Ellen," Molly replied without hesitation. "Jenny's mother. If anyone knows what's happening, it'll be her."

"Thank god you have her number," Max said, his heart swelling with relief.

As Molly held the phone to her ear, waiting for Ellen to pick up, Max paced the room, his mind a whirlwind of thoughts and fears. An uneasy silence hung in the air, broken only by the faint sound of Molly's breath and the distant hum of traffic outside.

"Hello?" The woman's voice on the other end was low, roughened by years of hard living and carried the weight of exhaustion.

"Ellen," Molly whispered, her words hushed but urgent. "It's Molly. Listen, something's happened to Jenny. We need your help. Jenny . . . She's been arrested."

A beat of silence, and then: "What?"

"For conspiracy to commit robbery," Molly replied, swallowing bile as she choked out the ludicrous charge. "The FBI stormed into her apartment at four in the morning, dragged her out in her pajamas."

Max paced restlessly beside her, his gaze flicking from Molly to the window where the faint light of dawn crept between the curtains. His fingers clenched and unclenched, betraying his own struggle to process the nightmare unfolding before them.

"Have you heard anything?" Molly asked, her heart pounding against her chest.

"Nothing," Ellen admitted with a rasp. "I had no idea . . ."

"Neither did we," Molly reassured her, the anguish in her face mirroring Max's. "But we're going to find out what happened. We won't let them take her away without a fight."

"Thank you," Ellen breathed, and the gratitude in her tone was heavy, almost palpable. "I'll try to get some answers on my end as well."

"Please do," Molly urged, her resolve steeling with each passing second. "We need to figure this out before it's too late."

"Too late for what?" Max inquired, unable to contain his concern any longer. Molly glanced at him, her expression a storm of emotions—determination, fear, and the barest flicker of hope.

"Before they take everything from her," she replied softly. "We have to act fast, or Jenny might lose more than just her freedom."

"Keep me updated," Ellen instructed, her tone suddenly firm with resolve. "And I'll do the same."

"Of course," Molly agreed, pressing her lips together as she ended the call. She met Max's gaze, and the unspoken understanding passed between them—a promise to fight for their friend, no matter the cost.

"Let's get to work," Max said quietly, with dark determination. The sun had begun its slow ascent over the horizon, casting long shadows that stretched across the room. Time was running out, and they both knew it—the race had begun.

CHAPTER
TWENTY-ONE

INSIDE THE QUINCY COURTHOUSE, a bailiff led Jenny through the maze of corridors until they reached the courtroom where her arraignment would take place. The air hung heavy with the scent of old wood and leather, imbued with the acrid tang of anxiety and despair. Rows of wooden benches stretched out behind her, unyielding witnesses to countless tales of misfortune and injustice. A few curious onlookers sat scattered among them, their gazes boring into Jenny's back.

Up at the front, an imposing judge's bench dominated the room, a silent sentinel of authority. To its left, the prosecutor's table was neatly arranged, papers stacked and pens poised for battle. Jenny found herself guided to the right side of the room, where the public defender awaited her arrival.

Jenny's gaze swept over the assembled individuals. The judge, a stern middle-aged man with a sharp nose and graying temples, regarded her with the same unreadable expression he probably wore when delivering verdicts. Beside him, a bespectacled court reporter sat poised to capture every word spoken, fingers deftly dancing across her stenograph machine.

Across the aisle, the prosecutor stood tall and confident, his tailored suit a mark of his power within these walls. His piercing eyes seemed to dissect Jenny from afar, as if already measuring her guilt.

"Jenny Winters?" came a deep, melodic voice from behind her. She turned, meeting the gaze of the tall, statuesque woman with long black hair cascading down her back. Her sharp eyes held a glimmer of determination, a testament to battles fought and won. "I'm Sandra Cruz, your public defender."

"Hi," Jenny replied.

The public defender, a woman who appeared to be in her mid-forties, had a calm presence and steady hands. She met Jenny's gaze, offering a reassuring nod before gesturing for her to take a seat beside her.

"Ms. Winters, we'll begin shortly," she said.

As the arraignment began, Jenny's thoughts raced. The courtroom came to life around her, voices rising and falling in steady rhythm as the legal dance unfolded. The prosecutor presented his case with an air of practiced confidence, and the public defender countered with a calm determination that seemed to emanate from deep within her core.

Jenny listened intently, her stoic veneer masking the storm beneath. In utter confusion, not recognizing herself in anything the prosecutor described, she realized she was just a pawn caught in the crossfire of this judicial chess match. She remembered the story in Sinclair's novel of the Italian anarchists who had been framed for murder back in the 1920s in a case fabricated by the judicial system. Her eyes dull with hatred, she realized some things don't change. But what didn't make sense is how she had landed on anyone's blacklist. She had done nothing that could make her look like a threat to the system.

In the wake of the arraignment, Jenny found herself escorted to a small, dimly lit conference room adjacent to the courtroom with her lawyer. The walls, plastered with water-stained wallpaper, seemed to close in on her as she shuffled across the worn carpet. A single overhead light cast an eerie glow over the scattered papers and legal documents that lay strewn across the table. This was to be the stage for her next battle.

"Let's get started, shall we?" Sandra said, pulling out a chair and motioning for Jenny to sit. As they settled into their seats, Sandra began to sift through the stacks of legal documents, her fingers deftly navigating the pages. "These are the charges against you," she continued, sliding a copy of the indictment across the table.

"Conspiracy to commit robbery," Jenny muttered, her heart pounding in her chest. "But I didn't do it. I didn't do anything. I literally just go to work and go home every day."

Sandra studied her for a moment, assessing her sincerity before nodding slowly. "That's what we'll prove," she said, firm and resolute. "Now, let's go over the details of the case."

As they delved deeper into the intricacies of the alleged crime, Jenny found herself drawn to the way Sandra carried herself. There was a quiet confidence about her, a sense of unwavering tenacity that seemed almost contagious.

"Jenny, I want you to tell me everything that's happened over the last month," Sandra said, leaning forward and resting her elbows on the table. "Don't leave anything out."

Taking a deep breath, Jenny began to recount anything she thought might be significant, but the sheer uneventfulness of her life left her grasping for anything to contribute to the case.

"Alright," Sandra said, nodding thoughtfully as she jotted down notes on a legal pad. "We'll need to analyze the prosecution's evidence and see if there's anything in your experience we can line it up with."

"Thank you," Jenny whispered, her chest tightening with gratitude.

In moments, the two women were escorted back to complete the arraignment.

Jenny entered a plea of not guilty.

After that surreal exchange with the judge, Jenny's gaze darted around the courtroom, taking in the austere wooden benches and the imposing judge's bench, before settling on the prosecutor. He stood at his table, a crisp suit barely containing his restless energy, as he pleaded with the judge for a speedy trial.

"Your Honor," he implored, "the backlog of cases in our court system is staggering. We must move forward with this case to alleviate the burden on our judicial resources."

The judge, an older man with a stern expression that seemed chiseled into his lined face, considered the prosecutor's words carefully. Finally, he nodded in agreement. "Very well. The trial will commence in two months."

Sandra's heart raced as Jenny's eyes met hers, both sharing the same sense of urgency. She knew that gathering evidence and building a defense in such a short time would be a Herculean task, but she refused to let fear take hold.

"Your Honor," Sandra interjected, "while we understand the need for efficiency, we request additional time to prepare for trial, given the complexity of the case."

"Denied." The judge was firm, leaving no room for negotiation. "Two months should be sufficient. We'll start the count after this week for the Thanksgiving break. The trial is set for January 16. Court is adjourned."

As the gavel struck the bench, Sandra led Jenny out of the courtroom and back to the small conference room where they had first discussed the case. They sat down, staring at the pile of evidence before them, as the weight of their task settled upon their shoulders.

"Two months," Sandra muttered, her brow furrowed as she calculated how to use every minute of their limited time. "We'll have to work around the clock, but I promise you, Jenny, we'll be ready."

Jenny watched as Sandra began sifting through the documents, searching for any nugget of information that could bolster their defense. She admired her lawyer's fierce determination, aware of the sacrifices she was making to help her.

"Thank you, Sandra," Jenny whispered, her voice barely audible. "I can't tell you how much I appreciate your help."

Sandra looked up, offering a tight-lipped smile as she acknowledged Jenny's gratitude, and the two women dove into their work, knowing full well that the clock was ticking, and each passing moment brought them closer to the trial that would determine the course of Jenny's life.

CHAPTER
TWENTY-TWO

JENNY SANK into the worn cushions of her couch, as if they could somehow absorb her confusion and fear. Her legs were pulled up to her chest, her slender fingers wrapped around her knees. The room felt both too big and too small at the same time, trapped in the paradox of a life that no longer made sense.

She stared blankly at the cracked plaster wall opposite her, but she didn't really see it. Instead, Jenny's mind raced, thoughts tumbling over one another like the waves of a stormy sea—anger, despair, disbelief, and, most of all, the desperate need to clear her name and find out who had set her up.

With a sudden burst of determination, she picked up her phone. As she dialed Max and Molly's numbers, the sound of the phone ringing filled the room. When their voices came through the line, tense and concerned, it was like a life preserver thrown to her.

"Jenny?" Max's greeting was a mix of surprise and worry, like he'd been expecting the worst.

"Hey, it's me," she replied. "I'm home on bail."

"Thank god," Molly breathed, genuine relief lacing her words. "What happened?"

"I was arrested and charged with conspiracy to commit robbery," Jenny said bluntly. The accusation still felt foreign on her tongue, an ugly stain that refused to be washed away.

"Jesus, Jenny," Max muttered. "I can't believe the judge bought that. Are you okay?"

"Can you guys come over?" she asked. "I need to talk."

"Of course," Molly agreed without hesitation. "We'll bring food."

"Thanks." Jenny hung up the phone and let it drop onto the cushion beside her, trying to steady her racing heart. The apartment felt smaller still, as though the walls were closing in on her, threatening to crush her beneath their weight.

***

The apartment door swung open to reveal Max and Molly, expressions etched with concern as their gaze swept over Jenny. She looked brooding and dangerous, the weight of her situation hanging heavy in the air around her.

"Hey, Jen," Molly said softly, arms laden with bags of Chinese takeout. Max followed behind her, his lanky frame appearing out of place in the small space.

Jenny hugged Molly in relief. "I'm so glad to see you. Where have you been? I was trying to reach you all last week."

Molly let out a sigh, her gaze distant. "It's a bit of a long story, but here it goes. So, remember the night you picked up your car and Eddie gave us that cryptic warning about Sean? Well, I decided to follow him. Big mistake. He somehow spotted me, and suddenly I found myself in a high-speed chase. I managed to lose him, but my luck didn't last long. I got pulled over by QPD for speeding, and things took a crazy turn."

Jenny's eyes widened with concern. "Oh no, what happened?"

"Believe it or not," Molly continued, "they mistook me for an undocumented immigrant and sent me straight to detention. I pleaded to call someone, but they refused. It was a nightmare."

Jenny's face showed a mix of shock and sympathy. "That's insane, Molly. How did you get out?"

Molly's expression turned grim. "Around five in the morning on Friday, an officer showed up out of the blue and said I was free to go. No explanation, nothing. I went back home and tried to make sense of it all. But then I realized something strange. They released me at the same time they were arresting you, Jenny. It can't be a coincidence, can it? And here's the thing: whatever Sean was doing in that parking garage, he really didn't want me to see him. I don't know what he would have done if he'd caught up to me."

Jenny cringed, looking like she was in physical pain. "Sean never told me anything about that. And I saw him the next day. And the day after that." She paused, grasping for some way to make Molly's story make sense in the world she thought she knew, involving the man she thought she knew. "Maybe it was someone else? Someone who looked like Sean from afar?"

Molly closed her eyes. "Very difficult to believe, honey. But we need to talk about you. What happened?"

"Tell us everything, Jenny," Max prompted, joining them at the table with a plate of steaming dumplings. "Start from the beginning."

So she did. She told them about the night she and Sean had hatched the pretend heist plan for her armored truck, a harmless game fueled by too many pints of beer. How they had sketched out the details on a napkin at the pub, laughing all the while, never dreaming that it could someday be used against them.

"But that's just it," Jenny said, worry gnawing at the edge of her words. "That napkin must have ended up in the hands of the FBI somehow. I just don't understand how."

"Maybe Sean knows," Molly suggested, her gaze sharp and searching. "He was there when you made the plan, right?"

"Right," Jenny agreed, though her heart clenched at the thought of involving Sean in this mess. She had come to see him as her partner in crime—figuratively speaking, of course —but now she wondered if he had somehow become tangled up in this confusion.

"Try to contact him," Max urged. "Ask him if he knows anything about how your plan got out."

"Alright," she said finally, determination surging through her veins. "I'll try to contact him. Maybe he can shed some light on all of this."

Jenny's fingers drummed impatiently on the tabletop as she pulled out her phone, scrolling through her contacts until Sean's name appeared.

"Here goes nothing," she muttered under her breath as she pressed the call button, the familiar tones of the phone ringing filling the room with an eerie echo.

As the phone rang, unanswered, each tone seemed to reverberate louder in her ears, heightening her anxiety. She leaned back against the couch, glancing between Max and Molly as if seeking some kind of silent reassurance. Molly gave her a tight-lipped smile, looking like she was trying to swallow a mouthful of needles.

"Hey, Sean," she said when his voicemail finally came on.

"It's me, Jenny. Listen, I need to talk to you about something important. Please call me back as soon as you can."

She ended the call and sent him a text message.

Sean, I really need to speak with you. It's urgent.

But the message remained undelivered, and Jenny felt a knot tighten in her chest. A sense of foreboding settled over her, her fingers tapping restlessly against the screen of her phone.

"Maybe he's just busy," Molly offered hesitantly, attempting to sound reassuring. "Or maybe he lost his phone."

"Or maybe," Max interjected, leaning forward, "he's not as innocent as we all thought."

Jenny bristled at his insinuation, her knuckles whitening as she clenched her fists around her phone. "What do you mean?"

"Look, I don't want to be the one to say it," Max began, in almost a whisper, "but what if Sean is involved in all of this?"

"Involved how?" Jenny demanded sharply.

"Remember when I told you that I saw Sean passing something to another guy in a parking garage?" Molly chimed in with concern. "It didn't seem like a friendly exchange. What if he was fencing stolen goods? Maybe even stealing valuable car parts from customer's cars at Eddie's Engines? And why did he chase me when he saw me?"

"Maybe," Max continued darkly, "he was using you to get insider information about armored trucks. To figure out how he could best rob one. If he knew he could get you to plan a pretend heist, then—"

"Stop," Jenny cut him off, her voice shaking despite her best efforts to remain composed. The thought of Sean betraying her trust, of using her as a pawn in some twisted conspiracy, was too much to bear. "You don't know him like I do. He wouldn't do that."

"Jenny," Molly said gently, reaching across the table to lay a hand on her arm, "we're just trying to make sense of all this. We care about you, and we don't want to see you hurt."

"I know," Jenny whispered, biting back tears. "But I can't believe that Sean would do this to me. There has to be another explanation."

"Maybe there is," Max conceded, more softly now, almost apologetic. "But for now, all we have are theories. And until we hear from Sean, there's not much else we can do. On the other hand, if he is the bad guy and the authorities have his phone, every time you try to contact him could be another piece of evidence they'll use against you."

Jenny crossed her arms over her chest, fingers digging into her skin as if grasping for something steady amidst the chaos swirling through her mind. Her gaze flitted between Max and Molly, searching their faces for any hint of doubt in their theory.

"Jenny," Molly began, softly but insistent, "I think we need to consider the possibility that Sean may have been using you to plan a heist for him."

"Using me?" Jenny's tone was laced with disbelief, and her lips twisted into a bitter smile as she shook her head. "You're talking about the man who took me out to dinner, out for drinks. The man who helped me fix my car when it broke down." Jenny lowered her eyes and her voice. "The man who slept with me. That's not the person you're describing."

"Maybe not," Max conceded, leaning back in his chair as he ran a hand through his hair, a tell that he was uncomfortable with the direction the conversation had taken. "But people can be two things at once, Jenny. It's not that far-fetched."

"Think about it," Molly interjected, meeting Jenny's eyes with a sympathetic intensity. "You work with armored trucks. You know the ins and outs of the job. Sean could have seen an opportunity and taken advantage of your knowledge."

"Plus," Max added, "you mentioned that you developed a pretend heist plan for fun with him. That's some pretty valuable information if someone wanted to pull off a real robbery."

Jenny felt her heart race as their words took root in her mind. She uncrossed her arms and began picking at her cuticles, a nervous habit she hadn't indulged in since she was a teenager. She scanned the room, as if trying to find something solid to ground herself, but everything seemed to blur together.

"Okay," she said finally, her voice barely audible, "let's say this is true. What does that mean for me? For us?"

"First and foremost, we need to find out what happened to Sean," Max said, his gaze unwavering. "And then we need to figure out how to clear your name. If he did use you, we need to prove it."

"Right," Molly agreed, a steely determination settling into her expression. "We're here for you, Jenny. We'll help you get through this."

Jenny struggled to reconcile the possibility that the man she had trusted may have betrayed her so deeply. Her breaths were shallow and uneven as Max paced in front of her. Molly leaned against the kitchen counter, arms crossed and lines creasing her brow. They looked like detectives in a crime drama, piecing together the motives of a cunning criminal. She never imagined she would be at the center of such an investigation.

"Jenny," Max began, his voice measured and steady, "It's

possible that Sean was arrested and then turned on you to get a better deal with the prosecutors."

"Wait, what?" Jenny blurted, her voice cracking with disbelief. "You're saying he sold me out?"

"Think about it," Molly said, stepping closer. "Sean could have been using you for information and then, when he got caught, he threw you under the bus to save himself. And that's why he isn't answering his phone: he's locked up."

"Or maybe he wasn't caught, but realized the heat was on," Max added, his sunken eyes reflecting a deep-seated fear. "Either way, we need to consider the possibility that he's thrown you to the wolves."

Jenny felt her stomach churn, bile rising in her throat as the implication of their words washed over her. They were suggesting that Sean had not only used her, but had betrayed her in the most callous and calculating way imaginable. She shook her head, unable to accept it. "No, no, that can't be true. He wouldn't do that to me."

"Jenny, you have to see the bigger picture here," Molly said, her voice earnest but gentle as she leaned forward on the couch. "The napkin with your heist plan, Sean's shady behavior, him going missing . . . it all adds up."

Molly's voice softened as she reached out to touch her friend's arm. "We don't want to believe it either, but the evidence is piling up. And if it's true, we need to protect you."

Jenny pulled away from Molly's touch, feeling both vulnerable and angry. How could they so casually suggest that Sean, the man who had once meant so much to her—being honest, the man who still meant so much to her—was capable of such a heinous act? She wrapped her arms around herself, as if trying to hold on to the remnants of her shattered trust.

"Maybe." Jenny hesitated, her fingers worrying the frayed

edge of the throw pillow she clutched to her chest. She looked out the window to the gathering darkness, the shadows creeping in like thieves, juxtaposed against the glow of the city beyond. "But it doesn't mean that Sean is necessarily involved in all this. There could be another explanation."

"Jenny," Molly sighed, "I know you care about Sean. But you need to protect yourself right now. You can't afford to blindly trust him."

"Exactly," Max echoed. "You're in enough trouble as it is. And if he really is mixed up in something illegal, being associated with him will only drag you down further."

Jenny bit her lip, her gaze fixed on the flickering streetlights outside. The world seemed to spin around her, and she felt adrift, unmoored by the possibility that everything she thought she knew was falling apart.

"Please," Molly implored, reaching out to lay a comforting hand on Jenny's arm, "just promise us that you'll be careful, and that you'll let us help you as much as we can."

"Alright," Jenny finally whispered. "I promise."

"Good," Max said, relief evident in his voice. He and Molly stood up, their faces etched with worry and determination.

"Get some rest, Jenny," Molly advised as she hugged her tightly. "We'll be here for you, no matter what."

Max embraced her as well, enveloping her in a cocoon of warmth and reassurance. "We've got your back, okay?"

As Max and Molly left, the door clicking softly shut behind them, Jenny sank back onto the couch, her thoughts churning. She tried calling Sean again, her fingers trembling as she pressed the call button, only to be met with the same frustrating result: ringing without end.

She stared at her phone, the screen casting a cold, blue light on her pale face, and wondered how everything had spiraled so quickly out of control. The echoes of Max and Molly's words haunted her, a chorus of warning and doubt that seemed to grow louder with each passing moment.

And as night fell around her, wrapping its dark embrace about the room, Jenny Winters knew that she couldn't escape the truth any longer: her world had changed, and there was no going back.

CHAPTER
TWENTY-THREE

SANDRA WORKED TIRELESSLY at her desk on Monday morning, just as she had the entire weekend. The stack of case files loomed over her, each one representing another obstacle in her path toward building a solid defense for Jenny. Witnesses were proving difficult to track down or unwilling to cooperate, and the evidence they required was scattered across various departments and offices, bogged down by bureaucratic red tape.

The critical witness, Sean Collins, had apparently disappeared. He hadn't responded to any of a multitude of texts and voicemails both she and Jenny had left for him.

"Damn," she muttered under her breath, rubbing her eyes as the weight of their predicament bore down on her.

"Any luck?" Jenny asked, watching Sandra from her seat across the room. She had been poring over her own set of documents, trying to find something—anything—that might help clear her name.

Sandra shook her head, frustration evident in the creases that deepened on her forehead. "It's like pulling teeth, Jenny.

I've sent out requests for evidence, but everything is slow going. And if we can't get people to talk to us, it's only going to make things harder."

"We need to consider every possible angle," Sandra continued, her voice measured and steady. "However unlikely, we must find someone who can help us prove your innocence."

Jenny let out a humorless chuckle, her gaze fixed on the papers strewn across the desk. "But we've tried everything, haven't we?"

"Almost," Sandra replied, turning to face her client. "There's still Sean Collins."

Jenny's heart lurched at the mention of his name. "Do you really think he'd help me? He hasn't even returned any of my calls."

Sandra sighed, rubbing her temples. "We don't have many options left, Jenny. If there's even a chance he can help us, it's worth pursuing."

"Fine." Jenny's jaw tightened, and she forced herself to meet Sandra's gaze. "If you think he can help, then I'll try again. But something tells me he won't come through."

"Let's not jump to conclusions yet," cautioned Sandra, returning to the cluttered desk. "For now, let's focus on what we do have: surveillance records, your statement . . . We need to make sense of all this evidence and somehow turn it against the prosecution's case."

"God, this is a mess," Jenny muttered, running a hand through her short hair. "Why did they ever target me in the first place? What do I have to do with any of this? I'm just a driver."

"Sometimes we get caught in the crossfire, Jenny," Sandra said gently. "But that doesn't mean we can't fight back.

Remember, we're in this together, and I won't stop until we've cleared your name."

Jenny nodded, though her expression remained clouded with doubt. "Thank you, Sandra."

Together, they continued sifting through the chaotic mountain of evidence, scouring each page for anything that could help their case. As they worked, Jenny felt a growing sense of desperation clawing at her chest—a gnawing fear that she would never be free from these accusations.

"If we can't get anyone to take our calls, then let's go talk to them in person," Jenny suggested, determination sparking in her. "We need to see the crime scene anyway, right? Maybe there's something still there that we missed. Something the police overlooked."

"Alright," Sandra agreed, sensing the urgency in Jenny's voice. "Let's visit the pub and see what we can find."

Afternoon light filtered through the cracked windows of the pub, illuminating the dusty corners and worn wooden floors. The air was heavy with the scent of stale beer and cleaning supplies, remnants of the night before when patrons had filled the space with laughter and camaraderie. Now, though, hushed after-lunch conversations hung in the air like smoke.

"Let's start at the bar," Sandra suggested, scanning the room with a practiced eye. "Maybe someone there remembers something useful."

A sense of unease slithered down Jenny's spine as they approached the bartender, a grizzled man with a bushy mustache who looked as if he'd seen his fair share of rough nights. She swallowed hard, trying to quell the nervous flutter in her stomach.

"Excuse me," Sandra began, her tone firm yet polite. "We're looking for information on a man named Sean Collins. My client was here with him a few weeks ago."

The bartender glanced between the two women, his face blank. "I see a lot of faces come through here," he grumbled. "Can't say I remember anyone by that name."

"Perhaps this will jog your memory," Jenny said, pulling up a photograph of Sean on her phone and sliding it across the bar.

The bartender studied the photo for a moment before shaking his head. "Sorry, can't help you," he replied, sliding the phone back toward Jenny.

Defeated, they moved from table to table, asking patrons if they recalled any conversations or encounters with Sean. Each response was the same: blank stares and shrugged shoulders, no recollection of the man whose testimony could change the course of Jenny's life.

"Time to try Eddie's Engines," Sandra suggested as they left the pub, the door swinging shut behind them with a heavy finality. "If Sean works there, Eddie should know how to contact him."

"Let's hope so," Jenny replied, her voice tight with anxiety.

They found Eddie Hanson in the back of his garage, grease-streaked hands gripping a wrench as he worked on an old car. He glanced up at their approach.

"Can I help you ladies?" he asked gruffly, wiping his hands on a rag.

"Mr. Hanson," Sandra began, "we're trying to locate Sean Collins."

"Sean?" Eddie's expression darkened, and for a moment, it

seemed as though he might refuse to answer. But then he sighed, casting his gaze to the floor. "Yeah, he worked here for a while, but he quit a couple of weeks ago. Left without a word, just up and vanished."

"Did he leave any contact information?" Sandra pressed. "An address, a phone number—anything that could help us find him?"

Eddie hesitated before shaking his head. "I'm sorry, but I don't have anything like that. Wish I could help, but he's long gone."

As they left the garage, the weight of their failed attempts to find a witness settled heavily on Jenny's shoulders. Her heart raced with fear and frustration, each beat echoing the dwindling chances of clearing her name.

***

Back in Sandra's cramped office, Jenny and Sandra hunched over the worn wooden table, its surface cluttered with photographs, documents, and spreadsheets. A dim desk lamp cast a sickly yellow glow, deepening the lines on their faces as they scrutinized each piece of evidence.

"Look at this," Sandra said, tapping the corner of a grainy surveillance photo taken from a street camera. "That's you walking away from the pub after meeting Sean."

Jenny stared at the image, haunted by the captured moment. "I can't believe they were watching me even then. I never thought I'd be a person of interest for the FBI." Her voice dripped with bitterness, unable to comprehend why she had been targeted.

"Tell me again about your involvement with any radical groups or political organizations," Sandra urged.

"None. Zero. Nada," Jenny insisted, frowning. "I'm in the union like everyone else at my job. That's it. No connection to anarchists, socialists, the Communist Party, or any other leftist group. As far as I know, I've never even met a communist."

Sandra slumped in her chair, pinching the bridge of her nose as she reviewed the evidence they had collected for Jenny's case. Beside her, Jenny absently drummed her fingers on the tabletop, her eyes hollow and ringed with fatigue.

"Okay," Sandra murmured, taking a deep breath and straightening up in her seat. "Let's go over our strategy one more time."

"Is there even a point?" Jenny snapped, her voice hoarse from hours spent rehearsing her testimony. "We're running out of time, and we still haven't found anything that'll clear my name."

"Jenny, we can't give up," Sandra responded, her conviction wavering only slightly under the strain. "Remember, you have a right to defend yourself, and I'm going to do everything I can to make sure you get a fair trial."

"Alright, let's focus on the opening statement," Sandra said, swallowing her emotions. "We need to emphasize your character, your dedication to your job, and the fact that this whole thing started as a joke gone wrong."

"Right," Jenny agreed, forcing herself to concentrate. "And when I testify, I'll explain how writing that heist plan was just me blowing off steam. It wasn't meant to be taken seriously."

"Exactly," Sandra nodded, scribbling some notes on a legal pad. "As for cross-examination, I'll prep you for the prosecutor's questions. You just need to remain calm and composed."

"Easy for you to say," Jenny muttered, her nerves fraying like worn rope. "You're not the one facing years in prison if this doesn't go our way."

"Jenny," Sandra said softly, reaching over to squeeze her client's hand with reassurance. "Trust me. I'm going to do everything in my power to keep that from happening."

"Thank you, Sandra," Jenny whispered, her voice thick with gratitude. "For not giving up on me."

"Jenny, I believe in your innocence," Sandra replied, looking into her eyes with unwavering conviction. "And we're going to prove it."

Jenny stared at the calendar pinned to the wall of Sandra's cluttered office. A red circle drawn around the date two weeks away seemed to pulsate with a malevolent energy.

CHAPTER
TWENTY-FOUR

THE COURTROOM WAS awash with a somber, almost austere atmosphere, as the sunlight streamed through the tall, arched windows and cast long shadows across the polished wooden floor. The judge's bench loomed at the front of the room, an imposing structure of dark wood and green leather upholstery, while the jury box, filled with twelve solemn-faced individuals, sat to the right.

A hushed silence filled the gallery where friends and family members of the defendant waited anxiously for the trial to commence. In their midst, Jenny Winters sat rigidly at the defendant's table, her petite frame swathed in a simple black dress. Her short hair framed a face drawn taut with tension, the corners of her mouth downturned and her jaw clenched.

Beside her, Sandra Cruz, Jenny's public defender, exuded an air of calm determination. Tall and statuesque, with long black hair cascading down her back, she wore a sharply tailored pantsuit that hinted at her keen mind. As she organized her papers and whispered reassuring words to Jenny, her gaze never wavered from the prosecution's table.

Jenny's mother, Ellen, sat in the front row of the gallery, hands clasped tightly together in a silent prayer for strength. She looked every bit the stalwart figure that Jenny had come to rely on, but behind the hardness of her gaze, there was a flicker of fear. She couldn't let Jenny see it; she had to be strong for her. Her lips moved silently in what seemed like a prayer for strength and guidance.

Max Thompson fidgeted in his seat, his hipster clothing contrasting sharply with the formal attire of those around him. Though he tried to maintain a nonchalant demeanor, his fingers drummed incessantly on his leg, betraying his anxiety. Seated next to Max was Molly Brown, dressed in a fashionable dress. She scanned the room, occasionally fixing on Jenny with a look of concern before flitting away to the rest of the court, as if sizing up the threat each person represented to her friend.

The judge, a stern older man with a hawkish nose and steely eyes, presided over the room from his elevated bench, gavel poised and ready to silence the whispers when the time came. He surveyed the gathering crowd, ensuring that order would be maintained throughout the proceedings.

In the jury box, individuals who had been called to judge Jenny's guilt or innocence shifted nervously, acutely aware of the magnitude of their words. They avoided eye contact, focusing instead on the polished wooden floor beneath their feet or the intricate designs engraved into the courtroom walls.

As the clock ticked closer to the appointed hour, the prosecutor strode confidently into the courtroom, a tall, wiry man with a sharp jawline and a no-nonsense air about him. His name was Arthur Brooks, and he had made a career out of putting away dangerous criminals.

"Order in the court," the bailiff boomed, and silence fell like a guillotine blade.

"Your Honor, ladies and gentlemen of the jury," began Brooks, his voice cutting through the hushed room, "today we are here to bear witness not just to a crime, but to a betrayal—a betrayal of trust and a flagrant defiance of the laws that bind our commonwealth together."

He paced before the jury box, locking eyes with each juror in turn. "The defendant, Jenny Winters, stands accused of conspiracy to commit robbery. A heinous act, no doubt, but it is not simply the nature of the crime that should concern us here today. It is the danger that she poses to our society, to the very fabric of law and order that we hold dear.

"Ms. Winters was entrusted with the responsibility of transporting our most valuable assets—assets that belong to each and every one of us as citizens of this great commonwealth. And yet, she chose to squander this trust, opting instead to plot and scheme in the shadows, in a betrayal of the people, and a betrayal of the employer who kept her on payroll, all for her own selfish gain. She is the very picture of an insider threat: the kind of person who would bite the hand that feeds them."

Brooks gestured toward the evidence table, where the prosecution's case lay in wait. "Over the course of this trial, we will present to you irrefutable proof of Jenny Winters's guilt, and we will ask that you uphold the values of justice and integrity that define our commonwealth by finding her guilty as charged."

The courtroom hushed as the prosecutor, Brooks, approached the evidence table. His fingers brushed against a clear plastic bag containing a crumpled napkin, marked with Jenny's messy handwriting. He held it up for the jury to see, his voice steady but charged with conviction.

"Members of the jury, allow me to present to you Exhibit A:

the very blueprint of betrayal. Upon this seemingly innocuous piece of paper, you will find a detailed plan outlining the heist Ms. Winters sought to execute—a plan that could have jeopardized the security of our commonwealth."

He placed the napkin back on the table and picked up another bag, this one filled with sheets of printed paper. "And here, Exhibit B: a record of Jenny Winters's internet search history. These pages reveal the extent of her meticulous planning: searches related to heists, anarchists, socialists, murder, and other nefarious information. They further reveal her motive in addition to financial gain—they show her to be a leftist extremist who seeks to rip apart the very economic and social fabric of our great nation, who seeks to destroy from within the family relationship that binds employers and their employees. One particular search you'll find most interesting: it was the inspiration for Ms. Winters's great crime. In this extremist literature, Ms. Winters learned of a payroll heist that took place in Braintree in the 1920s, in which two anarchists murdered the patriotic men who were transporting the cash to pay the wages of an entire factory of workers. Like Ms. Winters, they sought to steal the money those laborers had worked so hard to earn."

Brooks paused, allowing the weight of his words to resonate throughout the room. "Both of these items, along with further evidence that we will present today, paint a damning picture of the defendant's intentions." Even the air seemed heavy with implication, every breath drawn tainted by the specter of deceit.

"Your Honor," Brooks continued, turning toward the judge, "the prosecution would like to call its first witness: James Hartley."

As the courtroom awaited the arrival of the prosecution's

witness, a palpable sense of anticipation hung heavy in the air. Each person present was acutely aware of the weight of the impending testimony and the impact it could have on Jenny's fate. They sat, hearts pounding, breaths held, as the doors opened and the trial entered its next chapter.

The courtroom door opened with a measured creak, and in strode James Hartley, the prosecution's star witness. A tall man with short brown hair and deep brown eyes, he moved with the controlled grace of a predator, his tailored suit accentuating the lean muscularity beneath.

Jenny's breath caught in her throat as she recognized the man before her, not as James Hartley, but as Sean Collins, the mechanic who had charmed his way into her life. Her eyes widened, then narrowed with devastation and disbelief, twin fires of betrayal and rage flickering behind them. Beside her, Sandra Cruz sensed the shift in her client's demeanor and placed a steadying hand on Jenny's arm, ready to guide her through the storm that was about to break.

"Order!" The judge's gavel cracked like a whip, demanding silence from the gallery. His steely look bored into Jenny, a clear warning for her to keep her emotions in check as the proceedings continued. "Ms. Cruz," he said, voice low and firm, "please ensure your client remains quiet and composed."

Ellen Winters, Jenny's mother, gripped the edge of her seat, knuckles turning white, as she bore witness to her daughter's anguish. Her eyes welled with tears, unshed but brimming with a mother's fierce love and protectiveness. She glanced at Sandra, silently imploring her to defend Jenny against the web of deceit spun by the man now seated on the witness stand.

As James raised his right hand to take the oath, his expression was a mix of determination and unease—his eyes hard, his jaw set tight. He placed his hand on the Bible and swore to tell the truth, the whole truth, and nothing but the truth.

"Please state your name and occupation for the record," Brooks, the prosecutor, asked in a measured tone.

"James Hartley," he replied, a touch of reluctance in his voice. "I'm an agent with the Federal Bureau of Investigation."

A collective gasp filled the air, coming from the direction of Jenny's friends. Jenny gasped, and Sandra tensed noticeably.

"Agent Hartley, please tell the court about your investigation into Jenny Winters." The prosecutor's voice rang out with calculated authority. As James began to speak, his voice steady and assured, the courtroom seemed to collectively hold its breath.

"During my investigation, I posed as a mechanic at a local automotive shop where Ms. Winters brought her car for repairs." He paused, locking eyes with Jenny, who stared back at him defiantly, unwilling to give in to the crushing weight of his betrayal.

"Over time," he continued, "our relationship grew more personal, until she eventually confided in me her plans for a heist."

The prosecutor stepped closer to the jury box. "And did Ms. Winters express any extremist political views?"

"Objection!" Sandra sprang to her feet, her face a mask of righteous indignation. "Leading the witness!"

"Overruled," the judge intoned, his gaze never leaving James. "Proceed."

"Thank you, Your Honor." Brooks shot a satisfied grin at Sandra before turning back to James. "Please continue, Agent Hartley."

"Yes," James answered. "She expressed sentiments that are consistent with those of radical leftist extremists."

"And so that it's clear for the jury, what are radical leftists?"

"They come in a wide variety of flavors. Some of the more common are anarchists, socialists, and communists. They believe in the violent overthrow of the US government and of capitalism."

"Now Agent Hartley," the prosecutor continued, his voice crisp and clear, "please describe the evidence you gathered during your undercover investigation of Jenny Winters."

"Of course," James replied, his voice steady despite the havoc within. He looked down at the notes in front of him before launching into a methodical recitation of his findings. "I first made contact with Ms. Winters approximately three months ago while posing as a mechanic. I observed her behavior and quickly gained her trust."

The courtroom was still, each attendee hanging on James's every word. The judge leaned forward, his hands folded on the bench, while the jury members sat rigid in their seats, glancing between James and Jenny.

"During our time together, she confided in me a detailed plan to rob an armored truck from her place of employment," James said, his words measured and deliberate. "She described how she would gain access to the vehicle, disable its security measures, and make off with the funds without arousing suspicion."

Murmurs rippled through the gallery, punctuated by the occasional gasp or whispered exclamation. Jenny's mother Ellen gripped the edge of her seat, while Max and Molly exchanged horrified glances.

"Did she ever discuss her motivations with you?" Brooks pressed, his words slicing through the thick tension that hung over the room.

"Y-yes," James repeated, swallowing hard. The muscles in his jaw tightened as he forced the word out. "She did."

"Can you describe these conversations?" Brooks asked, his voice cold and clinical.

"Jenny said . . . she needed the money," James began, each word seeming to weigh heavily on him. "She was broke. She was in debt for car repairs and had a large debt with the IRS. She felt trapped, like there was no way out. She told me about the plan, how she'd researched it . . ."

"Objection!" Sandra interrupted, her face flushed with anger. "This is hearsay, Your Honor. The witness is merely repeating what my client allegedly told him."

"Your Honor, the witness is an FBI agent who was intimately involved with the defendant," Brooks countered. "His testimony regarding her statements is crucial to establishing her state of mind and motivations."

"Overruled," the judge declared, his gavel cutting through the heated exchange. "The witness may continue."

"Thank you, Your Honor," James said, his voice barely audible. He took a deep breath, steeling himself for what he would say next.

"Furthermore," James continued, his gaze locked on the jury box, "Ms. Winters attempted to convince me to join her in this endeavor, detailing how my skills as a mechanic would be invaluable in ensuring the heist's success."

"Objection!" Sandra interjected, her face flushed with anger. "Hearsay!"

"Overruled," the judge declared, waving a hand dismissively. "Continue, Agent Hartley."

"Thank you, Your Honor." James shifted in his seat, drawing a deep breath before proceeding. "In addition to her illicit plans, Jenny frequently espoused radical leftist extremist views during our conversations. She spoke passionately about her disdain for capitalism and the wealthy elite, and claimed that robbing a bank was simply a means of redistributing wealth to those who truly deserved it."

"Your Honor," Sandra objected again, "this is character assassination!"

"Overruled," the judge repeated, his voice firm. "The witness may continue."

As James recounted the details of their meetings and conversations, Jenny clenched her fists beneath the table, nails biting into her palms. Her heart pounded in her chest, each thud like a physical blow, as she struggled to comprehend the depth of his deception. She wanted to scream, to shatter the sterile facade that enveloped the room, but instead, she swallowed hard, forcing herself to remain silent under the judge's watchful gaze.

Through it all, she could not tear her gaze from James—the man who had betrayed her trust so wholly, who now sat mere feet away, calmly recounting under oath evidence he had invented himself. Jenny's eyes, once bright with defiance and hope, now shimmered with unshed tears that threatened to spill over. The courtroom seemed to close in on her, the walls pressing against her chest as she struggled to breathe. Her hands trembled beneath the table, betraying the storm of emotions that roiled within her.

"Thank you, Agent Hartley." The prosecutor offered a cold, professional smile as James finished his testimony. "Your insights have been most valuable."

"Ms. Cruz," the judge intoned, his voice heavy with expectation. "You may begin your cross-examination."

Jenny's heart hammered in her chest as she leaned toward Sandra, desperate to communicate the terrible truth to her lawyer. "Sandra, listen," she whispered urgently. "This agent—James—he's Sean. He's the one who . . . We were close." Her voice cracked with emotion. "He lied to me. He framed me. He made all this up."

"Miss Winters," the judge warned, his voice low and dangerous, "if you do not keep quiet, I will have no choice but to dismiss the witness and proceed without cross-examination."

"Your Honor, please allow me a moment to confer with my client," Sandra interjected.

"Make it quick, counselor," the judge replied, waving an impatient hand.

Sandra nodded curtly, then turned her full attention back to Jenny. "Tell me everything you know about him," she murmured, her gaze fixed on James as he shifted uncomfortably on the witness stand.

As Jenny recounted her relationship with Sean—or rather, James—her voice trembled with a mixture of anger and pain. Sandra listened intently, her face a mask of determination. When Jenny finished, Sandra straightened her shoulders and approached the witness stand, prepared for battle.

"Agent Hartley," she began, her voice steady and controlled, "isn't it true that while undercover as Sean Collins, you formed an intimate relationship with my client?"

James stiffened, his jaw tightening as he met Sandra's unwavering gaze. "My work required me to get close to her, yes. But it was strictly professional."

"Strictly professional?" Sandra's voice dripped with skepticism. "Did your professional relationship include spending time together at my client's home? Late-night conversations? Romantic dinners? Sleepovers?"

"Objection, Your Honor!" the prosecutor barked. "Leading!"

"Overruled," the judge muttered as he watched James squirm under Sandra's relentless questioning.

"Answer the question, Agent Hartley," Sandra prompted, her voice carrying an icy edge.

"Those interactions were part of my cover," James said evasively. "It was necessary to maintain the illusion."

"Was it also 'maintaining the illusion' when you suggested to Ms. Winters that she develop a pretend plan for a heist as a joke?" Sandra asked, her voice sharp with accusation.

"Absolutely not," James retorted, his face flushing with indignation. "I never suggested any such thing. All of my investigative techniques were legitimate and above board."

"Your Honor, I have no further questions for this witness," Sandra announced, her voice heavy with disappointment. She hadn't struck a home run, but she had at least raised some doubts in the jury's minds about the reliability of the witness.

As she returned to her seat beside Jenny, Sandra's mind raced with the implications of James's testimony. She had hoped to expose his betrayal, but instead, he had managed to evade her questions and defend his actions.

The prosecutor rose from his seat, a predatory gleam in his eye as he approached James on the witness stand. He wasted no time in launching into his follow-up questions.

"Agent Hartley," the prosecutor began, his voice cold and calculating, "is it true that during your investigation, it was necessary for you to gain the subject's complete trust for her to feel free to express her leftist opinions to you?"

James hesitated for a moment before answering, knowing full well the impact his words would have on Jenny's case. Finally, he replied, "Yes, it was."

"Would you say that these opinions were extreme, even by leftist standards?" the prosecutor pressed on, relentless in his pursuit to paint Jenny as a dangerous extremist.

"Objection, Your Honor!" Sandra interjected, her voice strained with desperation. "Calls for speculation!"

"Overruled," the judge declared, clearly growing impatient with the interruptions. "Answer the question, Agent Hartley."

"Based on my experience," James said carefully, "I would classify her opinions as extreme."

"Interesting," the prosecutor mused, circling James. "In your professional experience, Agent Hartley, do leftist extremists have a tendency to rob banks?"

"Objection!" Sandra cried out, her voice cracking under the weight of her client's fate. "Speculation!"

"Overruled," the judge stated once more, his tone final. "The witness may answer the question."

Taking a deep breath, James responded, "In my experience, yes. Leftist extremists tend to harbor resentment toward banks and the wealthy, often viewing them as symbols of oppression. Many of them don't believe in private property, so they don't see it as wrong to steal from banks—in fact, they don't even see it as stealing."

As James spoke, the jurors listened intently, their faces shifting from curiosity to outright disapproval. Some shook their heads in disgust, while others exchanged uneasy glances with their fellow jurors. It was becoming increasingly clear that they were beginning to view Jenny not as a desperate young woman caught in the crosshairs of an overzealous investigation, but as a dangerous radical who posed a threat to their way of life.

Jenny watched the jury's reactions, her heart sinking. She could feel the walls closing in on her, the weight of James's testimony and the jury's disdain crushing her spirit. For the first time since the trial had begun, she felt truly and utterly defeated.

"Thank you for your testimony, Mr. Hartley," the prosecutor said, nodding to James as he finished his damning revelation, his voice carrying a cold satisfaction.

"Agent Hartley, you are dismissed," the judge declared. His gavel struck the bench with an authority that seemed to resonate through James's very soul. He exited the witness stand, leaving behind the stunned faces of the defense.

Brooks turned to the judge. "The prosecution rests, your Honor."

"Very well," replied the judge. "We will reconvene tomorrow morning at nine o'clock. Court is adjourned."

The sharp rap of the gavel echoed through the chamber like a death knell. In the gallery, Jenny's mother Ellen closed her eyes, her face etched with despair. Max and Molly, their hands clasped tightly together, exchanged a look of shared heartbreak. They knew, as did everyone else present, that the noose around Jenny's neck had been drawn taut by none other than the man she had once trusted more than anyone: James Hartley, a.k.a. Sean Collins.

As the courtroom began to empty, murmurs spread among the attendees. Those who had come to witness the trial now spoke of the damning testimony they had heard and the seemingly irrefutable evidence against Jenny. It was clear that the tide of public opinion had turned against her, and few doubted the verdict that would be handed down the following day.

Jenny sat at the defendant's table, her once vibrant eyes now dimmed by the weight of betrayal. Her gaze had lingered on the retreating figure of James, as if searching for some semblance of the man she had known as Sean. But there was nothing left of him, only the cold, calculating agent who had used her for his own ends.

Jenny sat rigid, her face pale and drawn, her gaze fixed on some invisible point in the distance. Her hands trembled slightly at her sides. Sandra placed a reassuring hand on her shoulder, trying to ground her client amid the chaos.

"Take a deep breath, Jenny," she urged softly. "We'll get through this."

But Jenny barely heard her. Instead, she watched Sean—Agent Hartley—as he disappeared into the throng of people milling about the courtroom. Anger and betrayal pulsed through her veins, a bitter poison that threatened to consume her.

Sandra placed a hand on Jenny's shoulder, offering what comfort she could. "We'll fight this, Jenny," she whispered fiercely. "No matter what it takes, we'll fight."

But the words rang hollow in Jenny's ears, drowned out by the echoing sound of James's testimony and the tightening grip of despair around her heart. She knew that her life was now balanced on a razor's edge, and the odds were stacked against her.

As soon as the doors closed behind him, James stepped out into the crisp sunshine. He had expected to feel triumphant—this case would almost assure his promotion within the FBI. Instead, he was gripped by a hollow emptiness that threatened to consume him. That emptiness quickly descended into despair as he realized the depths to which he had fallen. The sun seemed to mock him, its warmth unable to penetrate the cold that had settled deep within his chest.

James leaned against the courthouse wall, feeling the rough texture of brick against his back. He closed his eyes, trying to escape the haunting image of Jenny's devastated expression as she recognized him for who he truly was—not Sean, her confidant and lover, but Agent Hartley, her betrayer. A sharp pain radiated through his chest as if his heart were cracking under the weight of his guilt.

He thought of how he had met Jenny at the mechanic's shop, how he had charmed her and won her trust. She had been just another assignment, a means to an end. But somewhere along the way, James had allowed himself to care for her—to see her as a person, not a pawn. And now, because of him, her life was unraveling before her eyes.

"Damn it," he muttered, raking a hand through his short brown hair. He could feel the ghosts of their shared laughter and whispered secrets lingering in the air, taunting him with memories of what might have been if circumstances had been different.

But there was no escaping the reality of what he had done. In his pursuit of career advancement, James had sacrificed an innocent woman's freedom. He could still feel Jenny's eyes burning into him, her gaze full of hurt and disbelief. The knowledge weighed on him like a millstone around his neck, dragging him down into the depths of his own self-loathing.

The sun dipped lower in the sky as James stood there, lost in his thoughts. He knew that this moment would haunt him forever—the price he had paid for ambition. The bitter sting of regret now overshadowed any hope for redemption, leaving him to wonder if the cost of success was truly worth the agony etched on Jenny's face.

"Sean . . . or should I call you James now?" Jenny's voice cut through his reverie.

He turned to face her, surprised to see her standing there, flanked by Sandra, who had a firm grip on her arm. Jenny's eyes were red-rimmed, but she stood tall, refusing to let him see her vulnerability. Her chin quivered, but only for a brief moment, as she bore down on him with all the anger and hurt she could muster.

"Jenny," he whispered, his voice barely audible. "I'm so sorr—"

"Save it," Jenny spat, interrupting him. "You lied to me. You used me."

"Jenny, please—" he began, but Sandra tightened her hold on Jenny's arm, drawing her attention.

"Stop," Sandra warned, her eyes flashing with anger. "You don't want to make things worse for yourself."

"Was it *all* just an act?" Jenny asked, ignoring her attorney. Tears threatened to spill from her eyes, but she blinked them back. "Did any of it mean anything to you?"

"Jenny," James pleaded, desperation creeping into his voice. "You have to believe me. I never meant for things to turn out this way."

"Enough!" Sandra snapped, pulling Jenny away from him. "Let's go."

As they walked away, Jenny glanced back at James one last time. The pain in her expression was almost too much to bear, and he looked away, unable to face the consequences of his actions.

Sandra's car doors snapped closed behind them, leaving James to confront the darkness that now enveloped him. He had crossed a line, and there was no going back.

The true cost of James Hartley's ambition became apparent, even to him. The lives forever altered, the hearts broken, and the dreams shattered—all in pursuit of a prize that, in the end, seemed to hold little value compared to the human wreckage left in its wake.

CHAPTER
TWENTY-FIVE

THE RED, white, and blue balloons bobbed above a large cake, its frosting emblazoned with the words "Justice Served" in bold letters. Streamers adorned every corner of the pale blue FBI office, reflecting the gravity of the occasion: the first day of Jenny Winters's prosecution. Colleagues shuffled into the room, their faces a mixture of triumph and relief.

"Where's James?" someone asked, interrupting the general chatter. It was true; Agent James Hartley, the man responsible for bringing Jenny to justice, was conspicuously absent from the celebration. His colleagues exchanged curious glances, unable to provide an answer.

"Maybe he's just running late," suggested a young agent, trying to fill the awkward silence that had settled over the room. She nervously shifted her weight from one foot to the other.

"Or maybe he's having second thoughts about the case," muttered another colleague under his breath, loud enough for those around him to hear. The comment caused a ripple of unease. James had been deeply invested in the investigation, perhaps too much so. His colleagues couldn't shake the nagging feeling that there was more to his absence than met the eye.

"Enough speculation," said Agent Thorn, clapping his hands together to regain control of the room. "Let's focus on the task at hand—celebrating our victory. James will be here when he's ready."

With that, the group tried to return to their festivities, cutting into the cake and raising glasses in toast. Yet the specter of James's absence loomed over them, casting a shadow on the otherwise jubilant atmosphere. They feigned laughter and camaraderie, but their attempts betrayed a shared concern that something wasn't quite right.

"Here's to James," said one agent, raising his glass in a toast. "May he find whatever it is he's looking for."

"Here, here," the others responded in unison, each hoping that their absent comrade would soon join them in celebrating the fruits of their labor. But as they continued to eat, drink, and make merry, the lingering question remained: where was Agent James Hartley, and why wasn't he there to partake in their celebration?

A subtle shift in the air drew Lauren Bernard's attention. She leaned forward, her eyebrows raised just a touch as she watched Agent Thorn take center stage amidst the celebratory chaos. His stocky frame cast a shadow over the red, white, and blue streamers that adorned the walls of the FBI office, his buzz-cut hair gleaming under the fluorescent lights.

"Listen up," Thorn's voice boomed as he addressed the room, "Since James isn't here to speak for himself, let me fill you in on some details of the case."

Silence fell over the gathering, and Lauren felt a flutter of curiosity in her chest. As Thorn began to recount the story of how James had gone undercover as a car mechanic, she scribbled notes furiously onto a notepad, her pen darting across the paper.

"James infiltrated the shop where Jenny was having her car repaired by posing as a mechanic named Sean Collins," Thorn explained with a hint of pride in his voice. "We got Eddie Hanson, the owner of the shop, to cooperate by threatening him with an IRS audit. You know how it is with these small business guys—they're all so unsophisticated that we don't even have to dig up any dirt on them. They practically hand us their own heads on a silver platter with the way they cook their books."

Lauren cringed at Thorn's mean-spirited comment, but she held her tongue, focusing instead on the way the other agents responded.

"Sounds like you had quite an operation going," remarked a bespectacled agent, admiration evident in his tone.

"Yep, it was a real team effort," Thorn agreed, puffing out his chest. "And now we've got Winters right where we want her."

"Too bad James isn't here to share the victory," another agent chimed in, her voice tinged with concern.

"James did his part," Thorn replied dismissively. "He's probably just off sulking somewhere—you know how he is."

Lauren bit her lip, suppressing the urge to argue. She knew there was more to James than met the eye, but she wasn't about to reveal her suspicions in front of Thorn and the others. Instead, she continued to jot down notes, capturing every detail of the story like a butterfly collector pinning specimens to a board.

As the agents continued to converse, sharing their perspectives on the case and toasting to their hard-won success,

Lauren couldn't shake the sense that something was amiss. She glanced around the room, taking in the forced smiles and worried glances that passed between her colleagues.

"Speaking of James," Thorn continued, his voice taking on a note of derision, "you all should know how close we came to having this whole operation blown wide open." He leaned against the edge of the table, crossing his arms over his chest as he surveyed the room. The FBI agents exchanged glances, their curiosity piqued.

"Jenny's friend Molly decided to play detective one day and followed our boy James. She managed to catch him meeting with an informant in a parking garage." Thorn shook his head slowly, smirking at the story.

"Wait, so what happened?" asked an agent, leaning forward with interest.

"James had to think fast," Thorn explained, his forehead creasing as he recalled the tense situation. "He couldn't risk letting Molly tip off Jenny about the investigation, so he convinced the Quincy Police to pull her over. Then he had ICE send them a request to hold her in immigration detention for a while. Gave us enough time to make sure everything was in order before we moved in on Jenny."

"Wow, that's . . . intense," another agent muttered, rubbing the back of his neck as he absorbed the information.

Lauren stared at Thorn, her pen hovering above her notepad as she struggled to process what she'd just heard. She could feel her heart pounding in her chest, the unease that had been simmering beneath the surface now threatening to boil over.

Around her, the other agents seemed similarly unsettled by Thorn's revelations. Despite their earlier bravado, the reality of the methods employed to bring Jenny to justice weighed heavily on them. There was a palpable tension in the room, a sense that everyone was reevaluating the price of victory.

"The important thing is that he got Jenny," Thorn said dismissively, clearly unfazed by the doubts clouding the faces of his colleagues. "And he did it without any interference from her little friend."

As Thorn's words echoed in the room, Lauren felt a chill run down her spine. It was as though she was witnessing the unraveling of a tapestry, each thread pulled revealing a darker, more troubling picture beneath. She knew that justice was often a messy affair, but there was something about this case— something about the way Thorn spoke of James's actions with such casual disregard for the law—that left her feeling cold.

"Of course," Thorn continued, leaning back against the edge of the table with the air of a man who had just finished recounting a particularly amusing anecdote, "Molly has no idea we were involved in her arrest. She probably thinks it was all just a big misunderstanding." He chuckled, but the sound was hollow and devoid of mirth.

"Seems like a bit of a risk, doesn't it?" ventured one agent, a young woman with glasses perched on her nose. "I mean, if she ever finds out . . ."

"Come on now," Thorn interrupted, waving a dismissive hand. "You really think some low-class townie like her is going to sue for wrongful detention? Nah, she'll just be grateful they let her go and won't ask any questions."

"Townie or not, Molly's still a person," another agent chimed in, his voice soft yet firm. "And people have a way of surprising you."

"Exactly," Lauren interjected. "We shouldn't underestimate anyone. All it takes is one determined individual to bring everything crashing down."

"Relax," Thorn replied, a smirk playing at the corners of his mouth. "This whole thing will blow over soon enough. We've got Jenny, that's what matters. And we did it without Molly blowing our cover."

"Still," the young agent persisted, "it seems like we're cutting it awfully close. What if she starts asking questions? What if she starts digging?"

"Then we'll deal with that when the time comes," Thorn said, his voice hardening. "But for now, let's just focus on what's important: Celebrating our success and bringing Jenny to justice."

The agents nodded, but the unease in the room was palpable. They clinked their glasses together, sipped lukewarm, nearly flat champagne, and tried to shake off the weight of their collective conscience.

"Here's to doing whatever it takes," Thorn declared, raising his glass in a toast. The other agents followed suit, though their expressions were sober, their hearts heavy with the burden of what had been done.

"Whatever it takes," they echoed, the words lingering in the air, haunting the celebration and casting doubt over their victory.

"Thorn's got a point," Agent Reardon hesitated, rolling the stem of his wine glass between his fingers. "We did what we had to do. It's not like Molly is completely innocent. Who is?"

"Still," another agent chimed in, her voice tinged with doubt, "it feels different when we arrest someone who didn't commit a crime."

Their gazes settled on Lauren, who sat in the corner of the room, her brow furrowed, her pen racing across the pages of her notebook. Her mind raced just as quickly, piecing together the events and weighing the potential consequences.

"Lauren?" Agent Kim called out, seeking her input. "You've been awfully quiet. What are your thoughts on all this?"

She paused, pen hovering above the paper, and looked up at her colleagues. Their faces were a mix of concern and defiance, a shared unease swirling beneath the surface.

"Thorn's right," she said slowly, her voice measured. "We can't let fear dictate our actions. But we also need to be prepared for any backlash. If Molly starts digging, we need to be ready."

The agents nodded, taking her words to heart. They knew the stakes were high, that the line between justice and deceit was blurred—and yet they held onto the belief that their actions were justified.

"Come on, everyone," Agent Kim said, clapping his hands together in an attempt to lighten the mood. "We're here to celebrate, remember?"

Nods and half-hearted smiles emerged as agents tried to shake off their unease. They gathered around the large cake at the corner table, the swirls of red, white, and blue icing a stark contrast against the pale blue walls. Streamers and balloons danced lazily in the air, evoking memories of childhood celebrations, a bittersweet reminder of simpler times.

"Where do you really think James is?" Agent Kim asked softly, his words barely audible over the sound of cake being cut and plates being passed around.

"Who knows?" Agent Thorn replied dismissively, taking a bite of cake. "Probably just couldn't handle the pressure."

Lauren pursed her mouth at Thorn's comment but kept silent. She knew better than to reveal her growing concern for James's well-being. It was a sentiment shared by many in the room.

"James knows what he's doing," Lauren finally said, picking at the frosting on her cake. "I'm sure he's just taking some time to think things through."

"Let's hope so," Agent Kim agreed, glancing around at their colleagues. "The prosecution might need him on the stand again, after all."

The celebration continued, but the agents' laughter and small talk felt strained, like a tightrope stretched thin over a chasm of doubt. They moved with caution, the weight of their actions bearing down on them, a constant reminder of the fragile balance they had struck. The unease that had threatened to consume the celebration now lingered in the air, a silent witness to the choices they had made—and the consequences that would inevitably follow.

CHAPTER
TWENTY-SIX

THE DARKNESS in James's apartment hung heavy. He sat slumped on the couch, his body weighed down by the crushing burden of his conscience. He stared at the lukewarm glass of whiskey beside him, willing it to dull the edge of his shame. But no amount of liquid courage could erase the memory of Jenny's face when she realized the extent of his betrayal. Her eyes, once vibrant with life, had turned dull and hollow as they bore into his soul.

He had done it all for ambition, to prove himself worthy of his badge and the respect of his superiors. Yet, what good was a career built on deceit and manipulation? How could he call himself a man of justice when he had entrapped an innocent woman in a web of lies?

He thought back to his superior officer, who had been eager to lock up a communist, to make an example out of her. James had taken advantage of that eagerness, fabricating evidence and manipulating Jenny into creating a heist plan she never intended to execute. It was a cruel joke, one that had spiraled out of control, leaving Jenny's life shattered and James's own sense of self hanging by a thread.

His heart raced as the enormity of his actions settled upon him. The stakes were high, but deep down, beneath the layers of guilt and regret, there was a flicker of hope. Perhaps it wasn't too late to do the right thing, to salvage some shred of dignity and possibly save Jenny from the injustice he had perpetrated.

With trembling hands, James picked up the phone, hesitating for a moment before dialing Sandra Cruz's number. Jenny's fierce and determined attorney, Sandra was the only person who might be able to set things right. As the phone rang, James's breath caught in his throat. Admitting his sins would come at a great cost, but he could no longer bear the weight of his deception.

"Hello?" Sandra's voice, sharp and alert, cut through the darkness.

"Hi, Sandra. It's . . . it's James Hartley." He forced the words out, his voice barely above a whisper.

"Agent Hartley? What can I do for you?" There was a note of suspicion in her tone, as if she sensed something amiss.

"I need to . . . I have to tell you something, about Jenny's case." His heart pounded in his chest, the words tumbling out in a rush. "I've done something terrible, and I can't live with it any longer."

There was a brief silence on the other end of the line, before Sandra replied, her voice steady, "Alright, James. Tell me what's going on."

As he took a deep breath and braced himself for the confession that would change his life forever, James knew that there was no turning back. "Jenny . . . she never planned that heist." James swallowed hard, his voice laced with regret. "I tricked her into creating the plan as a joke and turned it in to my superior officer as evidence."

Sandra's shock reverberated through the silence that followed. He could almost hear the gears turning in her sharp mind as she struggled to make sense of his confession. When she finally spoke, her voice was laced with restrained fury.

"James, do you understand what you've just admitted to?" Sandra's tone was icy, sending chills down his spine. "You set Jenny up, and now she's on trial for something she would never have done on her own?"

He felt the weight of her words crushing him, the guilt overwhelming. "Yes," he whispered, his voice barely audible. "That's exactly what I did."

"Listen to me, James," Sandra said, her concern for Jenny driving her to action, her tone one of a handler approaching a rabid animal. "If you truly want to make amends, you need to testify in court to what you've just told me. You need to tell everyone what you did, so we can save Jenny from this nightmare."

His hand trembled as he gripped the phone tighter, knowing that agreeing to testify would change everything. It would mean the end of his career at the FBI, and likely criminal charges against himself, but it was the right thing to do—and it might be the only way to repair the damage he had caused.

"Alright," he agreed, his voice firm despite the fear that twisted in his gut. "I'll do it. I'll testify."

"Good," Sandra replied, her voice softening slightly. "Thank you, James. This won't be easy, but it's the only chance we have to save Jenny."

A gust of wind rattled the windowpane as James sat hunched over his laptop. The screen's cold glow illuminated the stark lines of his face as he typed out his testimony, every sentence a nail in the coffin of his career. Sandra's voice drifted through the speakerphone, offering suggestions and asking probing questions that helped him to shape his words with precision.

"Make sure you describe in detail how you manipulated her into creating the plan," Sandra said, her voice a mixture of determination and concern. "The jury needs to understand the full extent of your involvement in the creation of the most important evidence against her."

James nodded, fingers tapping against the keyboard as he detailed his deception. He described the moment he had persuaded Jenny to sketch out the heist plan as a joke. He wrote about his superior officer's intense desire to make an example of a communist, and how that eagerness had allowed him to fabricate evidence without raising suspicion.

"Alright, I've added that in," James said, his voice heavy with regret. "Anything else?"

"Read it back to me, from the beginning," Sandra instructed, her tone firm yet empathetic. James obeyed, his voice cracking as the weight of his actions bore down upon him. After several minutes of tense silence, James finished reciting his testimony, and Sandra let out a slow breath.

"Good," she whispered. "This should be enough to help Jenny. Send it to me, and I'll prepare everything for tomorrow."

"Okay," he replied, swallowing hard. As he hit send, James realized the magnitude of his decision—testifying for the defense would not only cost him his future at the FBI but also tarnish his reputation beyond repair. Yet, the thought of doing right by Jenny compelled him to continue. "Thank you, Sandra," he whispered into the speakerphone, his voice filled with gratitude and determination. "I'll see you in court tomorrow."

"Take care, James," she replied softly, before ending the call.

James opened a new document, his fingers hovering above the keys. This time, he began to write his resignation letter.

"Dear Agent Thorn," he typed, the letters appearing like a silent confession. "It is with a heavy heart that I submit my resignation from the Federal Bureau of Investigation, effective immediately . . ."

As James wrote, the terrible churn in his stomach grew more and more intense. Finally, his resignation complete, he leaned back in his chair, staring at the damning words on the screen. Tomorrow, he would face the consequences of his actions—both for Jenny and for himself.

James hesitated for a brief moment, his finger hovering over the send button. The screen glowed with an eerie luminescence, casting his face in stark relief as he contemplated the weight of his decision. He scanned the text of the letter again, as if trying to absorb the finality of his choice.

Dear Agent Thorn,

It is with a heavy heart that I submit my resignation from the Federal Bureau of Investigation, effective immediately. In recent weeks, I have come to realize that my actions have not always been in alignment with the values and principles that this organization seeks to uphold. Specifically, the case involving Jenny Winters has called into question my own integrity and commitment to justice.

I wish to take full responsibility for my role in her entrapment, and I recognize that my continued presence within the Bureau would only serve to tarnish its reputation. It is with profound regret that I must walk away from a career that once meant everything to me. However, I am determined to make amends for my mistakes and strive toward a future guided by the principles of truth and justice.

Sincerely,

James Hartley

With a swift motion, James finally pressed the button, sending his resignation into the digital ether. As the "message sent" notification appeared, he felt a curious mixture of dread and relief wash over him.

The weight of his decision melted into the heavy air that lingered in the small, suffocating space of his apartment. James stared at the faint outline of the window, its panes obscured by the darkness outside. The muted glow of streetlights beyond painted a dim portrait of a world that seemed to be slipping away from him.

He exhaled slowly, contemplating the future that awaited him—one where his name would be forever tarnished by his actions and the lives he had affected. Ruined. That was what his reputation would be. All those years of hard work and dedication crumbled beneath the weight of a single choice. But it was a choice he knew he had to make, for Jenny and for himself.

"Jenny," he whispered, the name feeling foreign on his tongue as he dared to voice it aloud. It was her life that had been upended by his deceit, her trust that he had shattered. And yet, despite the darkness that threatened to consume him, there was a glimmer of hope that flickered within—a hope that, perhaps, he could make amends.

With a slow, deliberate movement, James reached out and switched on the lamp beside him. The sudden brightness stung his eyes, but he welcomed the pain, as if it were a physical reminder of the path he had chosen. The shadows retreated to the corners of the room, revealing the scattered remnants of his former life—files and documents strewn across the floor, an empty coffee cup stained with bitter memories perched atop a pile of discarded papers.

It was time to move forward. To step away from the wreckage he had created. James pushed himself up from the sofa, the fabric protesting beneath his weight. He stood tall, taking in the disarray of his apartment—a physical manifestation of the turmoil that had plagued him for so long. It was here that he would begin the process of rebuilding, brick by painstaking brick.

The door clicked shut behind James, sealing away the debris of his former life. For a moment, he stood there on the threshold, taking in the crisp Boston air that nipped at his cheeks and rustled the leaves of the trees lining the sidewalk. He gazed down the street, past old brick buildings crowned with snow, their windows glowing with warm light. A new beginning awaited him out there, somewhere among the labyrinth of city streets.

"Excuse me," a neighbor muttered, jostling James back to the present as he squeezed past him.

"Sorry," James mumbled, stepping off the stoop and onto the frosty pavement. A soft crunch echoed beneath his boots, affirming that he had indeed stepped into a new world. His breath clouded before him as he ventured deeper into the city, headlights casting fleeting shadows across his haunted face.

"Hey man, spare some change?" a homeless man slurred from the recesses of a doorway.

"Sorry, I don't have any on me," James replied apologetically.

"Good luck out there," the man called after him, his words trailing off.

"Thanks," James whispered, more to himself than the man he left behind. His thoughts turned inward, wrestling with the enormity of the task before him. Testifying for the defense would not only expose his own misdeeds but also cast doubt on the integrity of the FBI itself. The weight of his decision bore down upon him, threatening to crush the fragile foundation upon which he now stood.

CHAPTER
TWENTY-SEVEN

"YOUR HONOR," Sandra Cruz stood up from her seat, her voice steady despite the tension that filled the room. "The defense calls Mr. Eddie Hanson to the stand."

Eddie Hanson's heavy boots echoed through the courtroom as he made his way to the witness stand. The mechanic, a mountain of a man with sun-darkened skin and calloused hands, stood at the edge of the witness box. His broad shoulders were encased in an ill-fitting suit jacket that seemed to constrict his movements. The tension in his jaw was palpable as he raised his right hand. His eyes briefly met Jenny's, who sat silently at the defendant's table. There was a flicker of sympathy in his gaze before he took his oath and settled into the witness chair.

Sandra approached Eddie, her heels clicking against the floor with quiet authority. All around them, the courtroom spectators leaned forward in anticipation, curiosity piqued by the appearance of this new witness.

"Mr. Hanson," Sandra began, her tone professional yet

warm, "Can you please tell the court your role in the events leading up to my client's arrest?"

As Eddie recounted his involvement with the undercover operation, Jenny's thoughts raced. She remembered the small hints Eddie had given her about Sean's true identity, his subtle attempts to warn her of the danger she was in. Despite his initial cooperation with the FBI, it seemed Eddie had grown to regret his part in the trap they had set for her.

"Mr. Hanson," Sandra began, her voice steady and calm, "did Agent Hartley ever threaten you in any way to cooperate with his undercover operation?"

Eddie's face hardened as he recalled the encounter. He hesitated for a moment and swallowed hard, his Adam's apple bobbing beneath the starched collar of his shirt. "Y-yes, he did," he finally confessed, his voice barely audible.

"Could you please share the nature of that threat with us?" Sandra pressed, her gaze unyielding.

"He . . . he said that if I didn't help him, he'd make sure I got audited by the IRS." Eddie's voice cracked on the last few words, as if the mere thought of that possibility was enough to shatter him from within.

A collective gasp rippled through the courtroom, followed by a chorus of murmurs. The spectators, once passive observers, now leaned forward in their seats, their eyes wide with disbelief. Even the stern-faced judge seemed taken aback, his gavel hovering in mid-air as if he had forgotten its purpose.

Jenny's heart raced in her chest, her breath coming in ragged gasps as she tried to process Eddie's revelation. All this time, she had believed that he had betrayed her willingly, but now she saw the truth: he too had been a pawn in James Hartley's twisted game.

As the murmurs grew louder, the defense attorney raised

her hand for silence. "Ladies and gentlemen of the jury, we have just heard Mr. Hanson's testimony that Agent Hartley threatened him into cooperation. This information is crucial to understanding the context in which my client, Ms. Jenny Winters, found herself ensnared."

"Order," the judge finally intoned, his voice a sharp command that cut through the room's uneasy atmosphere. "We will have order in this courtroom."

As the tumult subsided, Jenny's fingers tightened around the edge of the wooden railing in front of her. She could feel the eyes of the jury on her, their expressions a mix of shock, sympathy, and suspicion.

"Your Honor," Sandra continued, her voice smooth as silk even as her demeanor belied her determination, "we must consider the implications of Mr. Hanson's testimony for my client's case. It is now clear that she was not the only one manipulated by Agent Hartley, and we cannot ignore the possibility that others may have been coerced as well."

As the trial resumed, Jenny felt a flicker of hope ignite within her chest. Perhaps, she thought, there was still a chance for justice to be served.

"Please," Sandra prompted Eddie, her gaze never wavering, "tell us exactly what Agent Hartley said to you, and how he delivered the threat."

Eddie hesitated for a moment, glancing briefly at Jenny before looking back at Sandra. "He walked up to me with this confident swagger," he recalled, his voice growing quieter as he delved into the memory. "His eyes . . . they were cold, calculating. Like I was nothing more than a pawn in his game."

A shiver ran down Jenny's spine as she listened, her heart pounding in her chest. It was as if the walls of the courtroom had receded, replaced by the dimly lit interior of Eddie's repair shop—its greasy floors and the scent of oil hanging heavy in the air.

"Go on," Sandra urged, her tone patient but insistent.

"James—or Sean, whatever you want to call him—leaned in close, so his face was just inches from mine," Eddie continued, swallowing hard. "He said, 'You're going to help me with my little investigation, Eddie. You don't want the IRS crawling all over your repair shop, do you? You've been cutting corners, and we both know it.'"

The courtroom remained silent as Eddie's words hung in the air, their significance not lost on those present. Jenny's grip tightened on the armrest, her knuckles turning white as she pictured James—the man she had once trusted—delivering that cold, calculated threat. As for the jury, it seemed their hatred of communists was trumped only by their hatred of the IRS.

"Finally, Mr. Hanson," Sandra said, her voice steady, "could you please describe James Hartley's involvement in the undercover operation? Specifically, any tasks or instructions he gave you?"

Eddie nodded, taking a deep breath. "James made it clear that his main goal was to gather evidence against Jenny. He wanted me to keep my eyes and ears open, report back to him about anything that seemed suspicious or out of the ordinary. He wanted me to tell him anything I knew about Jenny's friends and family—what he called her 'associates.'"

As he spoke, Jenny could almost see the scene unfolding before her: the dimly lit repair shop, the smell of oil and grease lingering in the air, the quiet menace in James's bearing as he issued his commands. Her heart ached with the weight of it all, a dull throb that threatened to consume her from within.

"Was there anything specific that he asked you to do?" Sandra prompted, her gaze never leaving Eddie's face.

Eddie hesitated for a moment, his jaw working as if the words were bitter on his tongue. "He wanted me to plant a listening device in Jenny's car, so that he could monitor her conversations," he admitted, his voice heavy with regret. "I . . . I did as he asked, but I never felt right about it. It felt like I was betraying her trust, even though I barely knew her. He also required me to look the other way when he lied to her about the repairs on her car. The car was ready, but he wanted to keep it in the shop longer to give himself more time to get close to her."

As Eddie continued to describe his interactions with James Hartley, the air grew heavy with anticipation, each word painting a picture of a man caught between loyalty and fear, manipulated by forces beyond his control.

"Thank you, Mr. Hanson," Sandra said softly, nodding toward the judge as she stepped back from the witness stand.

When he was finally dismissed, Eddie's eyes met Jenny's once more before he rose, his shoulders slumped beneath the weight of his confession. Jenny's mind raced with the implications of his testimony. She could feel the jury observing her, their expressions a collage of shock, sympathy, and suspicion. The atmosphere in the courtroom had shifted, each revelation sending ripples outward to touch every person present.

In that moment, Jenny felt a strange kinship with the man who had been both her friend and her betrayer. As the trial dragged on, she clung to the hope that the truth would set them both free.

CHAPTER
TWENTY-EIGHT

THE COURTROOM SHIMMERED with an almost palpable tension, as if the air itself were a tightrope stretched to its limit. The walls, adorned with elaborate woodwork and imposing portraits of past legal luminaries, bore witness to the unfolding drama. A hush descended upon the room as the bailiff called out the defense's next witness.

"Agent James Hartley, please take the stand."

He emerged from the throng of spectators, his tall frame rigid with apprehension. His short brown hair lay slick against his head, and though his face was nearly expressionless, it was clear that something within him was wavering.

The air in the courtroom seemed to constrict as James took the stand for the second time, this time testifying for the defense. The murmur of surprise rippled through the gallery, whispers and exchanged glances converging in a shock that hung heavy over the proceedings. Even the judge's gravelly voice faltered as he bid James to swear his oath once more.

"Permission to approach the bench, your Honor?" barked Brooks, the prosecuting attorney.

"You may approach," the judge replied. Both attorneys walked up to the judge.

"Agent Hartley is our witness," Brooks whispered urgently. "The defense can't call him. He's not on their list."

"Your Honor, we can consider this a recall of the prosecution's witness," responded Sandra. "It makes no difference to the defense what we call him."

"That's fine with me," conceded the judge, "and Brooks, there's no reasonable argument against recalling the witness."

Defeated, the prosecutor returned to his seat and Sandra approached the witness box.

"Please raise your right hand," the bailiff commanded, and James complied. "Do you swear to tell the truth, the whole truth, and nothing but the truth, so help you God?"

"I do," he replied, his voice resonating through the hallowed chamber.

As he settled into the witness chair, his gaze fell upon the small but powerful figure in the defendant's seat. Jenny Winters, her straight hair framing her pale face, stared back at him with bright eyes that seemed to bore into his very soul. He couldn't shake the feeling that she knew the turmoil brewing within him—the same turmoil that had haunted him since their paths first crossed.

"Agent Hartley," began Sandra Cruz. Her voice was calm, yet assertive. "You are here to provide testimony in the case against Ms. Jenny Winters, is that correct?"

"Yes," James affirmed, struggling to maintain his composure. As he spoke, the first time he had met Jenny came to mind, when he posed as a mechanic under the alias Sean Collins. Their connection had been immediate.

"Mr. Hartley," said Sandra Cruz, her heels clicking against the polished wooden floor as she approached the witness box. "You've already testified for the prosecution, correct?"

"Yes," James replied, voice strained. A bead of sweat trickled down his neck, betraying his turmoil as he fought to balance duty and desire.

"Then why are you here, testifying for the defense today?" Sandra asked, her tone a blend of curiosity and challenge.

"Because . . . I have more to say," James admitted, glancing at Jenny. Her eyes shimmered with uncertainty, but also an ember of hope that refused to be snuffed out. He steeled himself, knowing that these next words could either save or destroy her.

"During my investigation of Ms. Winters," he began, his gaze never leaving Jenny's, "I manipulated her into creating the heist plan."

Gasps filled the courtroom, the truth crashing like waves against the shore, threatening to sweep away all that had been built on lies.

"Explain," Sandra demanded, her grip on her notepad tightening.

"Under my alias as Sean Collins, I gained Jenny's trust," James continued, his voice wavering between guilt and resolve. "I used our relationship to gather information about her vulnerabilities, her financial struggles, her fear of losing everything. I planted the idea to plan a heist in her mind and nurtured it with my words and actions."

"During your investigation," Sandra continued, "did you engage in any activities that could be considered . . . unethical?"

James hesitated for a moment, the weight of his choices bearing down upon him. He knew what he had to do—uphold the law and reveal the truth. But as he looked at his boss,

Agent Thorn, he couldn't shake the desire to protect himself from the consequences of his own actions.

"Objection," said the prosecutor, sensing James's hesitation. "Calls for speculation."

"Overruled," replied the judge, his voice stern but not unkind. "The witness may answer."

Taking a deep breath, James looked into Jenny's eyes one final time before speaking. The words hung heavy in the air, and as they left his lips, he knew there was no turning back. "I engaged in an intimate relationship with the subject of the investigation."

"Throughout this process," Sandra prompted, "did you ever think about the consequences of your actions? How they might affect Ms. Winters?"

"Every day," James admitted, his voice barely more than a whisper. "I knew what I was doing was wrong, but . . . I felt trapped by my duty to perform for the FBI. To conduct a successful investigation and bring about an arrest."

"Your duty," Sandra repeated, her tone laced with bitter irony, "to manipulate an innocent woman into committing a pretend crime and frame her for it?"

"Yes," James breathed, his chest tightening as he confessed his sins. The room seemed to fade away, leaving only him and Jenny locked in a silent battle between love and betrayal.

The hush within the courtroom weighed heavily, as if a thick fog had descended upon its occupants. Sandra Cruz, Jenny's unwavering attorney, stood with her shoulders squared, her jaw set in determination.

"Your honor," Sandra Cruz began, addressing the presiding judge, "given the new evidence presented, I move to have the charges against my client dismissed with prejudice on the grounds of no probable cause, lack of evidence, and mistakes in the criminal complaint."

A murmur suffused through the room, prompting the judge to raise his gavel slightly, poised for order.

Jenny's heart pounded under her ribcage, threatening to betray her stoic exterior. She could feel the weight of the stares from the jury, the prosecution, and the spectators; each gaze probing, scrutinizing, seeking signs of guilt or innocence in her every breath.

"Agent Hartley has testified," Sandra continued, her voice imbued with focused passion, "that he manipulated my client into devising the heist plan. He preyed upon her vulnerabilities, her financial struggles, exploiting them to serve the interests of his investigation."

The sound of shuffling papers and shifting bodies filled the room, as tension thickened the atmosphere. Jenny watched as the prosecution glanced nervously at their notes, their faces twisted with the realization that their case was slipping through their fingers like sand.

"Your Honor," Sandra pressed, turning to face the judge, "the very foundation of our legal system rests upon the principle of a fair trial. Entrapment and framing, or making up this case out of nothing, as orchestrated by Agent Hartley, has violated that principle and tainted these proceedings beyond redemption. My client has done nothing wrong, has broken no law."

The judge's lined face remained inscrutable, but the angry expressions of the jury members seemed to echo the turmoil in Jenny's chest. They looked like people who had just realized they'd been played for fools. As the room held its collective breath, Jenny wondered if her fate would be decided by the moral compass of a single man.

The judge regarded Sandra thoughtfully. His stony gaze alternated between Sandra and the prosecution, weighing the validity of the argument before him. Jenny observed the scene unfolding, her heart pounding relentlessly in her chest.

"Mrs. Cruz, do you have any further evidence to support this claim?" the judge asked, his voice steady and authoritative.

Sandra nodded, quickly producing a stack of documents from her briefcase. "I do, your honor. These documents outline the steps taken by Agent James Hartley during his investigation, including several instances of direct manipulation and coercion of my client."

Jenny's hands clenched tightly in her lap. She watched as the prosecution team exchanged uneasy glances, their once-confident demeanor now wavering under the weight of James's testimony.

The judge took the papers from Sandra, scanning through each page meticulously. As he read, the courtroom remained eerily silent, the tension in the room palpable. Every tick of the clock seemed to echo throughout the hallowed chamber.

"Prosecution, how do you respond to these allegations?" the judge asked, his gaze piercing through the opposing counsel.

"Your honor," stammered the lead prosecutor, his face flushed with embarrassment, "we were not aware of these actions by Agent Hartley."

"Clearly," the judge replied sharply. "I will take this motion under advisement and give my ruling tomorrow morning. Court is adjourned for today."

With a sharp rap of his gavel, he signaled the end of the day's proceedings—but not the end of Jenny's uncertainty. As the courtroom emptied, she found herself rooted to her seat, watching Sandra Cruz collect her papers with a determined intensity that seemed to radiate from her very being.

"Jenny," Sandra said softly, approaching Jenny and placing a comforting hand on her shoulder. "We'll reconvene tomorrow. Get some rest."

"Thank you, Sandra," Jenny murmured, her voice barely audible amidst the cacophony of footsteps and whispered conversations.

"Of course," Sandra replied, giving her shoulder a reassuring squeeze before departing with a purposeful stride.

Jenny took a deep breath and allowed herself a glimmer of hope for freedom. As she left the courtroom, she could feel the eyes of those who had followed the trial upon her, their gazes heavy with questions and suspicion. But she held her head high, refusing to let them see the cracks in her armor, even as her heart continued to fracture under the strain of betrayal and uncertainty.

CHAPTER
TWENTY-NINE

JENNY SAT motionless on the edge of her seat, a desperate tension filling her limbs like a caged animal. The weight of the entire trial hung heavy upon her slender shoulders, and she clung to the hope that justice would prevail.

The judge entered the courtroom with an air of grave determination. He settled into his chair, arranging his black robes around him before addressing the court.

"Based on the new evidence presented and the testimony of Agent Hartley," he began, his voice steady and authoritative, "it is clear that Ms. Winters was subjected to entrapment and falsification of evidence by the FBI."

Jenny's heart caught in her throat, her breath hitching as she struggled to comprehend the judge's words.

"Accordingly," he continued, "I am compelled to agree with the defense's argument. The charges against Ms. Winters are hereby dismissed."

The courtroom shuddered with the weight of the judge's decision, each set of eyes widening with shock and disbelief. The lead prosecutor clenched his fists and ground his teeth in frustration, while his younger associate stared blankly at her legal pad, her fingers trembling as she gripped her pen.

"Objection!" Brooks barked, but the judge waved him off with a stern glance.

"Your objection is noted, counselor," the judge said, his voice resolute. "However, my decision stands."

In the gallery, FBI agents exchanged wary glances, their faces taut with tension. Lauren, James's fellow rookie, bit her lip. She knew the implications of this outcome, not only for James but also for the entire bureau.

"Order in the court!" the bailiff shouted, trying to restore a semblance of calm as the room buzzed with hushed conversations and rustling papers.

"Ms. Winters, you are free to go," the judge declared, directing his attention toward Jenny.

"Thank you, Your Honor," she replied, her voice firm yet subdued.

For a moment, time seemed to stand still. Then, as if propelled by a force outside of herself, Jenny rose unsteadily to her feet. She could hardly believe what had just transpired; after months of torment, anguish, and uncertainty, she was finally free.

Tears welled up in her eyes, spilling over and tracing hot trails down her pale cheeks. She felt a hand on her shoulder, and turned to find Sandra, her face flushed with pride and satisfaction.

As Jenny turned to go, Sandra Cruz offered her a warm, proud smile. "Congratulations, Jenny," she whispered, her own eyes glistening with emotion. "You're free to go."

"Thank you," Jenny managed to choke out between sobs. "I owe you my freedom."

"It's been a privilege," Sandra replied, a fierce determination evident in her gaze. "Now let's get you out of here."

Together, they made their way through the throng of onlookers, each step a declaration of Jenny's reclaimed freedom. As they made their way toward the exit, Jenny caught a glimpse of James in the crowd. His face was a mask of anguish and disbelief, his eyes clouded with regret. It was his testimony that had ultimately saved her, but at what cost?

"Jenny!" he called out as she approached the door, desperation seeping into his voice. She hesitated for a moment, her heart heavy with conflicting emotions.

"Go on," Sandra urged gently, giving her a reassuring squeeze. "You're safe now."

With a nod, Jenny resumed her stride, pushing through the heavy oak doors that separated her from the world outside. As they swung shut behind her, the cold wind of a late autumn afternoon greeted her like a long-lost friend. She lifted her face to the sky, letting the chill air kiss her cheeks as she reveled in her newfound liberty.

James burst through the courthouse doors, his heart hammering in his chest as he scanned the bustling street for a glimpse of Jenny's retreating figure. He spotted her a few yards away, her eyes shining with unshed tears as she moved gracefully through the crowd.

"Jenny!" he called out again, desperation clawing at his throat. "Please, wait!"

This time, she stopped. For a moment, it felt as if the world stood still—the cacophony of car horns and murmured conversations fading into nothingness as she turned to face him.

"Let me explain," James implored, his voice cracking with emotion. "I was just doing my job. Or what I thought was my job."

"Your job?" Jenny repeated, incredulity laced in her words. She stared at him, her gaze cold and unyielding, as her hands clenched into fists at her sides. "You ruined my life, James. And for what? A paycheck? A promotion?"

"Jenny, I never meant for any of this to happen," he said, taking a step toward her. "I didn't want you to get hurt."

"Didn't want me to get hurt?" she scoffed, her lip curling in disdain. "Well, congratulations. You failed spectacularly."

"Please," he whispered, pleading for understanding. "I'm sorry."

"Sorry doesn't change anything," she hissed, her words like icicles piercing his heart. "You betrayed me, James. I trusted you, and you played me for a fool."

The wind picked up and howled through the streets, whipping lashes of hair across her pale cheeks and carrying with it the echoes of their shattered past. In that moment, James knew there was nothing he could say to make amends; no words would ever be enough to mend the chasm that had opened between them.

"Goodbye, James," Jenny said, her voice barely audible above the din of the city. And with that, she turned away from him once more, her back straight and proud as she strode toward an uncertain future.

As the sun dipped below the horizon, casting long shadows on the cold concrete beneath his feet, James Hartley found himself truly alone.

CHAPTER
THIRTY

AFTER A SURREAL JOURNEY, Jenny finally entered the dimly lit lobby of her apartment building, the scent of old carpets and damp plaster clinging to the air around her.

"Hey, Jenny," Max called out, his voice tempered with warmth. Beside him, Molly beamed, her arms laden with takeout containers and a bouquet of flowers that seemed to capture the hues of twilight itself.

"Hi, guys," Jenny replied, her words edged with surprise. "What's all this?"

"Consider it a little pick-me-up," Molly said, her eyes twinkling with mischief. "We thought you could use some company."

As Jenny approached them, Max and Molly stepped forward, their arms opening wide. They pulled her into a tight group hug. Jenny felt the tension in her chest loosen.

"Thanks, you guys," she whispered, her words muffled by the fabric of Max's flannel shirt. The earthy scent of his cologne mingled with the faint smell of fried food from the takeout boxes.

The trio navigated the dimly lit hallway, their shadows spilling over the worn carpet as they made their way to Max's apartment. A dim light seeped through the crack beneath the door, casting a thin golden line upon the hallway floor. Max fumbled with his keys, finally unlocking the door and pushing it open to reveal his eclectic space that somehow reminded Jenny of an old-world library crossed with a makeshift artist's loft.

"Here we are," Max announced, ushering them inside. He set the beer on the counter while Molly arranged the food on the kitchen table.

"Max, this is . . . really thoughtful of you," Jenny said, her cheeks flushing with gratitude.

"Hey, what are friends for?" he replied, brushing off the praise with a casual shrug.

Molly deposited the takeout containers on the large, battered kitchen table, which was surrounded by mismatched chairs. The aroma of fried food mingled with the scent of old books and well-worn leather.

As they settled into the cozy space, plates piled high with steaming dishes, conversation flowed easily between them. With each shared laugh, the weight of recent events seemed to lift, leaving room for the comforting embrace of normalcy.

As they settled around the table, Molly cracked open a beer and took a long swig before setting it down and turning to Jenny. "So, I've been thinking," she began hesitantly, her fingers drumming nervously on the tabletop, "I'm pretty sure my detention was engineered by the FBI because I saw Sean having a covert meeting in the Kilroy Square parking garage. It can't be a coincidence after everything we know now."

Jenny blinked, taken aback. Being so consumed by her own case, she hadn't made that connection yet, but it made sense.

Her thoughts turned inward as she recalled her own recent experiences, and a stark realization hit her: she had landed on the FBI's radar because of the internet search she'd done on anarchists and a payroll heist in Braintree that had happened over a hundred years ago.

"Wow," Jenny whispered, her voice barely audible as her mind continued to reel. "I'm pretty sure I got their attention for something even more ridiculous. You won't believe it."

"Try me," Molly said with an encouraging nod, leaning in closer.

"I searched online about some anarchists and a heist from way back when. I was trying to find the title of the Sinclair novel I've been reading. My mom told me about the plot, but I couldn't remember the title. That's it. It's insane they're surveilling people like that and opening investigations with so little to go on," Jenny said, shaking her head in disbelief.

Max's eyes widened as he processed what Jenny had just shared. "You're kidding," he said, running a hand through his hair. "That's . . . wild. I mean, you've barely even been to any protests. And neither of you are members of any political parties, right? Or am I missing something?"

"Exactly," Molly chimed in, her voice tinged with frustration. "The federal government is still so afraid of leftists that they're willing to target people like us? Honestly, it's absurd. Imagine the files they must have on real socialists."

Max spoke up. "Look, I'm no expert on government surveillance or anything, but it seems like they're grasping at straws here. You two don't pose any real threat, and they know it."

"Maybe," Molly mused, her fingers tapping a staccato rhythm against the table. "Or maybe they're just desperate to maintain control, even if it means going after people like us."

"Either way," Jenny sighed, pushing her empty plate away, "it's unsettling to know that we're being watched."

"Hey," Max said after a pause, "you know . . . my older brother's a litigator. I bet he could sue the FBI for both of you for what they've done." He looked from Molly to Jenny. "Imagine if you came out of this mess millionaires."

Jenny blinked at Max, her heart skipping a beat at the thought. A new life, one where she wasn't constantly struggling to make ends meet, seemed like an impossible fantasy.

Molly's face lit up with a mischievous grin. "Oh man, can you imagine? We'd be unstoppable! I'd start my own business and finally get out of the dead-end jobs I keep falling into."

"Really?" Jenny asked, her lips curving into a grin. "A business?"

"Absolutely," Molly laughed. "Something fun, like a vintage clothing shop or a cozy little bookstore. I'd finally be my own boss, and I wouldn't have to worry about money ever again. What about you, Jenny? What would you do if you became a millionaire?"

The question swirled in her mind, filling the small apartment with tantalizing possibilities. Would she travel the world, leaving her armored driver life behind? Or perhaps invest in her own business too, forging a new path entirely?

"To start, I think I'd buy my mom a house," Jenny said softly, the image of Ellen's tired smile and the way she always had Jenny's back coming to the forefront of her thoughts. "She deserves it, after everything she's done for me."

"Aw, that's sweet," Molly murmured, reaching across the table to give Jenny's hand a squeeze. "I'm sure she'd love that."

"Those sound like good dreams," Max said softly, his gaze lingering on Jenny for a beat longer than necessary before turning to Molly. "And who knows? They might just come true."

"Here's hoping," Jenny murmured, clinking her bottle against Molly's in a silent toast.

Molly glanced at her phone, her face falling as she realized how late it had gotten. "I should head out," she said reluctantly, rising from her seat.

"Let me walk you to the door," Jenny offered, following Molly.

"Promise you'll call me tomorrow?" Jenny asked as they reached the door.

"Of course," Molly replied, pulling her into a tight hug. "We'll get through this, okay? The worst has to be behind us, right?"

"Must be," Jenny whispered, releasing Molly and stepping back into the apartment, the door clicking shut behind her.

After a companionable few minutes clearing the table, Max rummaged through a kitchen cabinet. The dim light accentuated the lines of his jaw, and Jenny couldn't help but notice the way his broad shoulders filled out his shirt.

"Found it!" Max announced, triumphantly brandishing a half-empty bottle of whiskey. "I think we both could use a drink."

"Agreed," Jenny replied, watching as he poured two generous glasses. He handed her one, their fingers brushing briefly in the exchange. A small thrill ran up her spine, which she took note of inwardly, surprised by her own reaction.

"Cheers," Max said, raising his glass. Their glasses clinked together with a soft chime, and she met his eyes—warm, inviting, and undeniably attractive.

"Cheers," Jenny echoed, taking a sip of the amber liquid. It burned going down, but the warmth that spread through her chest was welcome after the emotional rollercoaster of the past few weeks.

They fell into an easy conversation until Jenny found it impossible to ignore her exhaustion anymore.

"Thanks for everything tonight, Max. It means a lot," Jenny said.

"Of course, Jenny. Anytime," Max replied, his whole manner softening, reflecting an unspoken understanding between them.

They embraced, bodies pressed together in a comforting cocoon of affection and newfound possibilities. As they pulled apart, Jenny promised to catch up with him soon before making her way upstairs to her apartment.

The door closed behind her with a gentle click, sealing off the world and its myriad uncertainties. The familiar scent of her sanctuary enveloped her like a reassuring hug, as she slipped off her shoes.

Jenny lay down on her bed, the soft sheets cradling her tired body. As she stared up at the ceiling, her mind replayed the whirlwind of events—the breakdown of her car, the relationship with Sean, which she now understood to have been an ongoing assault, Molly's disappearance, and her own arrest and trial. It all seemed like a fever dream, a surreal collection of memories that had been stitched together so haphazardly that couldn't possibly have really happened to her.

But through it all, there was Max—unwavering, dependable Max. And as she closed her eyes and surrendered herself to sleep, a slow smile bloomed on her lips.

ABOUT THE AUTHOR

Jules Spencer lives in Quincy, Massachusetts and worries too much about cyber surveillance. This is his debut novel.

ABOUT THE PUBLISHER

Sidewalk
Fiction Studio

Sidewalk Fiction Studio is an imprint of

Sidewalk Audio LLC

United States

www.sidewalkfictionstudio.com

www.sidewalkaudio.com

MORE FROM SIDEWALK FICTION STUDIO

Cry It Out by Kate Wollaston

In this domestic thriller, a young mother trapped in a carefully constructed deception must discover who the real threat to her baby is before she is forced to make an impossible choice.

Perfect Trust by Rowan Fields

When a fascinating stranger collapses on her beau's doorstep, a series of misunderstandings threatens our heroine's belief in their young love. Variations on the 1913 novel *Miss Mystery* by Etta Anthony Baker.

Tackhammer's Toy Shop by Wren Cox

When the mischievous fairy Bright Eyes sets her sights on the bored toys in Tackhammer's Toy Shop and decides to bring them to life, the magic and mayhem that follow threaten to ruin Christmas for the whole village.

www.ingramcontent.com/pod-product-compliance
Lightning Source LLC
Chambersburg PA
CBHW031038310726
48969CB00007B/2031